RIGHTING MY WRONGS

A GUARDIAN ANGELS MC NOVEL

TISHA S. STOW

This is a work of fiction. Names, characters, businesses, places, and events are either the products of the author's imagination or are used in a fictitious manner. Any resemblance to actual persons, living or dead, or actual events is purely coincidental. Mature audiences only.

Triggers warnings: suicide, child abuse, and rape

Cover Designer: Lou at LJDesigns

Model: Jonny James

Photographer: Wander Aguiar of Wander Aguiar Photography

I WILL LEARN TO LIVE IN
THE SUNSHINE OF YOUR
LIFE INSTEAD OF THE DARK
SHADOW OF YOUR DEATH.

-UNKNOWN

RIGHTING MY WRONGS

TANK

This party is in full swing, as we've just patched in our newest member. Crow started prospecting for us right before we took down the Devil, also known as Thorn McCormick, President of Hell's Fury. This club was once like Hell's Fury when it was run by my sorry-ass uncle. I killed him and the majority of his members after they killed my mother. I then took over and changed the name to Guardian Angels, far from the demons it was once called.

Thorn had a very large shipment of guns and drugs in a little house right outside of Tybee Island. Let's just say we hit that lick and kept on moving. Crow found us a buyer, who paid us more than we were expecting. We're already stable in the financial department, but it's safe to say we are set for life, as well as our kids and grandkids. The kid has shown his loyalty over the last year and earned his patch.

"Kid, be prepared to have more ass thrown at you than

you can handle with this kut on," I say, holding it up.

He slides his arms inside, pulling it up onto his back. The room goes wild. Clapping, hoots, and hollers of congratulations.

Of course, Navy has to throw in her two cents, "Yeah, Crow, just make sure none of that ass getting thrown your way is infected. Snoopy over here doesn't care either way, that's why he's always scratching. Nasty bastard." She looks over at Snoop, sticking out her tongue.

Snoop flips her the finger. "Fuck you, Navy."

She scrunches up her nose, shaking her head. "Ew, hell no, not even with Capone's dick." We decided over a year ago that Navy was one crazy bitch, but she's family and we love her crazy ass.

"Sis, did you take your meds today because that shit was not cool," Capone says with the same scrunched-up face. He claimed Navy as his sister from the beginning.

This is my family. I'll always have missing pieces, but I'm still one lucky bastard.

* * *

I'm about three sheets to the wind with Corset grinding on my lap when my phone rings. It's Dodger, our other prospect who's been with us for a little over a year as well. He's still a hesitant little shit though, but loyal to a fault. He tells me I have a visitor named Johnny at the gate. "I don't know a fucking Johnny. Get rid of him, Dodge."

I hear a commotion, before another voice comes on the phone, "You're gonna want to see me. Open the fucking gate, Tank."

I have no recognition of the voice, but I tell Dodger to go ahead and open the gate. If some fucker is coming to my home with my family trying to start shit, he's gonna have so many holes in his body no one will be able to recognize him.

"Shut that music the fuck off!" I tell the boys to load up and be out of sight just in case some shit pops off. As soon as I hear the banging on the door, I sling it open.

"This how it is now, Zane? I gotta jump through hoops to see you, old man?" Johnathan says.

I don't know if my mind is playing tricks on me because he and his mother have been heavy on my mind lately or if I'm actually seeing the kid I used to call my son standing in front of me, only now he's a grown-ass man.

"Johnathan?" it comes out as a whisper, but he hears me.

"Yeah, old man, it's me. Only, I don't go by Johnathan anymore. Just Johnny. Well, you gonna keep me outside in the cold or let me the fuck in?"

I'm shocked but slide to the side, letting him in. Memphis is beside me and speaks to Johnny, giving me time to get my head out of my ass, "Damn, kid, it sure has been a long-ass time. I think you were seven the last time I saw you." He motions him toward the bar. "I see you've lost that stutter. How's your mom?"

Memphis took the words out of my mouth. He remembers only them, not what they meant to me. Hell, he was just an eighteen-year-old kid who lost his parents and his mind afterward for a few years.

"That's actually why I'm here. I wanna prospect for the Guardian Angels. I need your protection when I go against the motherfucker hurting my mom and all of the assholes protecting him. I need you." He takes a minute to look around the room. "I need all of you at my back."

I see red, my blood boils, and all I can think about is getting to Layla and killing whoever is hurting her. "What the fuck do you mean? Who's hurting Layla?" I'm now pacing, no longer experiencing shock, only feeling anger.

That's why I left them over a decade ago, to keep them safe from people looking for me. I'm confused. Layla is a wonderful, sweet woman who would give her last. Why is someone hurting her? Why would anyone want to . . . Unless . . .

"It's not any of the Demons, is it? I killed the majority of them, but a few spread out around the map, hiding deep. I've never stopped looking for them, but haven't had any luck on their whereabouts either." If someone is hurting her because of me I wouldn't be able to take it, knowing I left to protect her only to have her hurt anyway. "Fuck!" I slam my fist into the wall probably breaking a couple of fingers. My is anger getting the best of me.

"Calm down, old man, shit. I see your temper hasn't changed at all over the years." Johnny grabs my shoulder with a hard squeeze.

I turn, giving him a big hug. "Damn, Johnathan, it's good to see you, son. I've missed you and your mom so much over the years."

His expression turns hard, and I have no idea what I've said to change his mood. I don't have time to dwell on it as

I whistle loudly, letting the boys know it's time for church.

They all make their way toward the room when Johnathan grabs my shoulder, turning me around. It's just me, him, and a few kut sluts left in the main room, but the sluts are too far away to hear his words, which is the only reason I don't put my foot in his ass and let him know whose house he's in.

"Don't ever call me your son again, Tank. You lost any right to that title the day you left us, leaving me to watch my mama cry day in and day out until she ended up with an even bigger piece of shit who beats and rapes her.

"I did, once upon a time, wish you were my real father, loved you like a father, but watching your mama break in your arms day after day changes your heart, hardens it. I learned a long time ago that once-upon-a-time shit is only for fucking fairy tales. The life we've lived is far from a happily ever after, old man.

"I need your help. I need these bastards taken out. If it was something I thought I could do on my own, trust me, I wouldn't be here." He walks away.

I let him . . . this time.

* * *

"All right, boys, first and foremost, let me introduce you to Johnny. I don't share a lot of my past with you guys for reasons I won't get into right now. I've gotten intel on Layla and Johnny throughout the years." I look over to see his eyes widen in surprise that I hadn't just forgotten about them. "Once she became involved with someone else, I stopped keeping close tabs due to other reasons I will not discuss with you gossiping bunch of assholes. Well that, and the fact that my intel guy became silent, almost as if he'd disappeared.

"Anyway, all you need to know is they are now and have always been family. They need our protection right now, and they'll damn well have it. Any questions?" I look at my brothers and see smiling faces all around the table. No one says anything, so I continue, "Okay, Johnny, what do we need to know about the piece of shit your mom is seeing?"

He looks around the table, all eyes are on him, waiting for him to speak. This is something he's not comfortable with because as soon as he opens his mouth his words get stuck, "H—he is a pol—police officer."

I hold my hand up, stopping him. "You have absolutely no reason to feel nervous or out of place here. In this room, we are brothers, family."

He nods his head but still looks like he might puke.

Capone speaks up, "Social anxiety is a bitch, bro, but nothing to be ashamed of, especially in here."

Johnny nods again, this time with a smile before he tells us his story, "He's a police of—officer. One of the dirtiest bastards in North Georgia. He's well known and pretty much untouchable. He's got cops and criminals in his pocket. If I'm right, and I feel in my heart that I am, they have a drug and prostitution ring they're running. I've wanted to kill him for a while now, but whatever he is holding over my mama's head must be serious because she won't let us get involved. The one time I tried, he arrested me, making it clear he would fuck up my record so I would never be able to go to college or get a good-paying job. He hurts my mom physically, mentally, and emotionally. I can't take her tears anymore; it's fucking killing me. I can't leave because I refuse to leave her behind with him so he can do God only knows what to her."

The more he talks, the madder I get. I can't take it, knowing someone is hurting her this way is getting the best of me. I don't know how much more I can listen to before I snap.

"He fucked a prostitute he arrested on our fucking kitchen table. He made my mom sit there while he did it."

I slam the same hand I hurt earlier down on the table. "No fucking more! Not right now. I can't hear any more of this shit. Who is this fuck? I need his name right now!" I'm yelling and pacing, but I can't sit still. My fingers hurt, my heart is beating so hard it feels like it could burst out of my fucking chest at any second. Why? How? Where did I go wrong? I should have stayed then this would never have happened to my angel.

"Byron Jamison is his name. He's good at playing the ever-loving and caring protector of the community. Hell, the day after he fucked a prostitute on our table, beat us bloody before locking us in the fucking cellar, they posted him in the damn paper. He was posing with a big-ass teddy bear and some kids. It was that "shop with a cop" shit. They make him out to be a hero when he's a fucking criminal— worse than a criminal."

The room is silent. Every brother has a face filled with pure disgust, loathing. One thing we don't like is the abuse of innocent women and children. That's the quickest way to get fucked up around us.

* * *

"Dane, I need everything you've got on someone, but before I tell you his name, I need to let you know that he's blue." I look around the table at all my brothers and Johnny as we wait in silence to see if he's willing to get info for us on one of his own.

"In my department?" he asks, sounding somewhat hesitant.

"Actually, no. This one is in North Georgia and the little intel I do have tells me he's a real shady son of a bitch. Dirty as they can get, with his hands in a little bit of any and everything illegal."

We don't have to wait long this time around. "Give me the name. If it's one thing I hate, it's a dirty-ass blue. I might give intel, but it's against fucking criminals—those who hurt innocents. I do not condone one of us using our badge of fucking honor for evil doings."

I admire that about him, but at the end of the day, he's still a cop. "Jamison. Byron fucking Jamison. I want everything you can get." I'm seething, ready to rip the motherfucker's head off.

"How did I know that name was going to leave your mouth? That piece of shit is just that. As is that whole fucking precinct. This won't be an easy task, Tank. Jamison has untraceable connections, no one knows who. He's probably one of the dirtiest cops I've ever seen but never faces consequences for his actions. Nothing, I mean absolutely nothing the man does is subtle. He is blatant in his actions, not caring one damn bit. So, if you're going toe to toe with him you're going to need some blues on your team. I'm on board and know just the right men to help out. Give me a couple of days and I'll have some information for you." He hangs up before I can say anything further.

Johnny's phone rings, causing us all to look his way. "I'm sorry, but I've gotta take this, it could be important." He jumps up, acting nervous. As he walks out the door, I hear him say, "What's wrong, B, is everything okay?"

LAYLA

"Where is the little bastard at, Layla? If you don't tell me, it's just going to make things so much worse on you when I get back home tonight." His grip tightens on my chin as he lifts me off of the ground.

I try to speak even though his grip is restricting my mouth. "I've already told you he went out to meet some girl he's been seeing. He should be home in a bit." He squeezes one more time before letting me go, causing me to fall to the ground. I know I'll have bruises around my face within the hour.

"You better pray you aren't lying to me because if you are, you already know what I can do." He walks out, slamming the door behind him.

"Dammit, Mom, why can't we just leave here?" My youngest son at fifteen has seen more than he should have ever had to. He's the spitting image of his father, which I love and hate.

"What have I told you about that mouth, boy? Don't cuss in this house. You ain't too big to get your ass whipped." I always say this to bring a smile to his beautiful face and, just like every other time, he laughs.

"Okay, shorty, whatever you say." He's already taller than me, which isn't hard to do at my 5'4. He gets his height from his dad, just like everything else. "Come on, woman, let's get you off of this floor and into that kitchen to cook your son some food before he wastes away to nothing. You feeling up to it, or are you hurting anywhere else besides your face?" He examines me as he pulls me off of the floor. "Mom, Johnny and I would kill him in a heartbeat if we could. You know that, right? He's got way too many people on his payroll though, too many threats have been made. I don't want to lose you, Mom." He hugs me tight.

"You won't lose me, baby, I promise. We will get away from this hell, hopefully, sooner than later. Now, let's go start that food before you starve to death."

His stomach growls in response causing us both to laugh.

"Where the hell is Johnny anyway? Have you talked to him yet, because he damn sure hasn't answered my calls?"

He quickly drops his smile and gives me some bullshit story about having something to do upstairs before dinner. I know those two are up to something, I just don't know what.

* * *

The fajitas are almost done when I hear a commotion outside. I run to the window, looking out to see Johnny having words with the officers Byron put here as a lookout to make sure we don't leave. I swing the door open to tell Johnny to get inside, but he's already standing in front of me. "Get your ass in this house, son. You know they're just going to call Byron to tell him every little thing that goes on here. We don't need to piss him off anymore than he already is."

He's staring at me with fire in his eyes as he observes my face. I'm sure he's seeing some pretty intense bruising that's beginning to show.

"Oh, we're definitely going to piss him off more than he already is," a beautiful girl with wild eyes says as she walks through my door with what looks to be a fucking butterfly knife covered in blood.

"Who the fuck are you?"

She smiles a sweet smile and introduces herself, "My name is Navy. I've got a feeling we're gonna be good friends. It's so nice to meet you, Layla." She reaches out her hand to shake mine, but rude or not, I don't know this crazy-ass woman.

"How do you know my son?" I cross my arms over my chest, doing my best to stand a little taller. Apparently, this is funny to not only Navy but my son as well.

"Mom, you need to calm down. Navy is a new friend of mine." He looks over at her, winking. "I think I'm gonna keep her."

She winks at him before giving him a peck on the cheek.

"Whoa now, little Johnny, don't try to move in on my ol' lady." A very large biker comes through my door, followed by a few more.

"You keep calm, Memphis, you know I'm all yours."

Memphis, Memphis, why is that name so familiar to me? I look at him trying to remember.

"It's been a long time, Layla. How are you?" he says.

And it clicks.

"No, no, no! Johnny! What did you do? Please look at me, son. Tell me you did not do anything stupid." I'm panicking. I turn to go back to the kitchen, so I can take my chicken off the stove but run straight into a hard body. I can't look up. I know that smell. It's like it was yesterday that he walked out my door.

"Hello, beautiful, it's so good to see you again."

Just like that, I'm thrown back almost sixteen years to a day my very soul was broken.

LAYLA

Sixteen Years Ago

"Just get the fuck out, Zane! You made your choice and it's not with us." I hear Johnathan's cries coming from the stairs, knowing he's eavesdropping once again on adult conversations. I know he loves Zane, but I have to protect us from him coming in and out of our lives whenever he feels it's okay, only to destroy us in the end.

"Baby, you aren't even listening to me. I love you and Johnathan. I want to be here with you, both of you. Please, just let me take care of this business so I don't have to worry about my past coming in and hurting either of you. I would never forgive myself if anything happened to you guys. Let me get rid of the threats and I'll be back."

I look at him, knowing how much I love him, but can't let him leave us. "It will always be this way, Zane. Anytime something comes up with the club you'll be gone again, right? I won't let you do this to us anymore. If you walk out that door it's forever this time." I see the turmoil in his eyes as I turn and walk away to go comfort my crying son.

"I love you, Layla." I hear him say right before the door closes, taking my broken heart with him.

LAYLA

"**L**ayla, are you okay?" He reaches down, putting his finger under my chin, lifting my face, and looking into my eyes. "You take my breath away, just like you did the first time I saw you all those years ago."

He does the same to me, but angers me more in this moment. Tears spring to my eyes and roll down my cheek.

"Please don't cry, beautiful. I'm taking you away from this place and all the pain that lives here."

I ball my hand into a fist, then swing, connecting with his jaw. "Get the fuck out of my house, Zane! All of you need to get out! Now!" I'm so angry, I'm shaking.

"Mama, why are you screaming?"

I hear a few oh fucks and a deep intake of breath behind me.

"Brady, get back upstairs until I come get you."

He doesn't move, because he's a stubborn little shit, which is one of the only things he did get from me.

"Brady? His name is Brady?"

I turn around to see Zane looking at Brady with such hurt in his eyes.

"Yes. Now, can all of you please leave my home?" I look around and see that someone has already packed bags for us—they're all on the living room floor.

Johnny walks over to me and pulls me into a hug. "It's time, Mama. We need them to get us away from that piece of shit. The only way that's gonna happen is if we get rid of him and everyone on his payroll. Plus, he deserves to know him, Mama. It's always bothered you that Brady didn't get to meet or know him."

One by one, each member grabs a bag and leaves. Navy, I think it is, gives me a quick hug. "It'll be okay, I promise. I came from a bad place when Memphis came into my life too. It will get better for you and your handsome boys. I can't believe how much he looks like Tank."

There is no denying Zane is his father because they look so much alike. I knew if he saw him once he would know.

"Mama, who are these people and why the hell do you look like you're about to cry again? Did someone else hurt you?"

I grab my boy and pull him close. "No, baby, these people are here to help us. Your brother already took your bag, so go on with him now so I can talk with Zane for a minute."

He looks over my shoulder at his father for what seems like forever before leaving the room. I'm afraid to turn around. Afraid of what's to come, but I know I have no choice. I wasn't prepared for the hate radiating off of him.

His voice, as well as my heart, breaks as he speaks his next words, "How could you, Layla? I've loved you for what seems like a lifetime. You've already ripped me apart once. What? Was that not enough for you? Now— wow . . . I can not believe that now you go and rip what's left of my fucking heart out of my chest only to leave me bleeding. How the fuck could you let me go almost sixteen years without telling me I had a son? A fucking son who is the spitting image of me at that age." He paces the room before speaking again, "I'm here to help because Johnny came to me. He knew exactly where to find me, Layla. But you couldn't tell me I had a son?

"I will get to know my son and, hopefully, get close to Johnny again, but after this motherfucker is dead and no one is left to hurt you, you can go back to doing whatever the fuck you want. You are not the woman I thought you were at all. The woman I loved would have never done this to me."

The last sound I hear is glass shattering. A picture falls off of the wall, hitting the ground, as he slams the door behind him.

TANK

They all ride in the cage with Navy and Memphis. Right now, with how I feel, it's a damn good thing they did because as bad as I want her behind me on my bike I don't trust myself around her. I would never put my hands on her in a negative way, but right now I'm mad as fuck, and sometimes I can't control my tongue. I mean, fifteen fucking years have passed. Years I can never get back. I don't know what his first words were or when he took his first steps. How can I get past this?

I try to calm myself, all the anger I feel, before pulling in at the clubhouse, but it's no use. I'm boiling at this point. My blood pressure is out of control if the heat and pressure around my head are any indication.

We all pull into the clubhouse, but I wait until I see everyone else start making their way in before dismounting my bike. I'm caught off guard by a hand gripping my shoulder, attempting to turn my body but falling short in the strength department. I turn to see my boy looking at me with nothing but pure anger.

"I may look like you, but I'm nothing like you. I would never leave my pregnant girlfriend to raise a child on her own." He points to where his mother and Navy are standing. "That woman over there has been a mother and father to me while you've been living it up with your club and your whores, so if you ever make her cry again I will beat your ass or die fucking trying. You got that, old man?" He pokes his finger into my chest before turning around, leaving me speechless, but proud as hell at the same time.

Until his words register that is.

My temples start to throb as anger takes over. Why the hell would she tell him those things? Like I just knew about him this entire time, but didn't give a shit? I think it's about time the baby mama and I had a fucking discussion. "Layla! My office, *now*!" I yell across the yard, making heads turn from every direction, but not giving two fucks about any of them.

* * *

Inside, pacing, preparing in my mind what needs to be said, the door opens and her beautiful face comes into view. I lose all train of thought.

"Don't you dare yell at me in front of all those people, Zane! I'm a grown-ass woman and you will not treat me like a child, nor will I be treated like one of your obedient little whores. Are we clear, asshole?" She comes in with that fire I love so much about her.

I'm confused as to why she can come out swinging at me, but allow that piece of shit boyfriend of hers beat and mistreat her. So, the next words out of my mouth are just that, which lead to her screaming, cussing, and eventually swinging at me until I have no other choice but to pin her hands behind her back with her face down on my desk.

Her beautiful, round ass is pressed into my very aware, very hard cock. "Shut the fuck up, Layla! Dammit, woman, can you not keep your mouth closed for five damn minutes? Since you're not gonna use it for a good cause, I'm asking you nicely to keep the damn thing shut."

She squeals loudly, bucking against my hold. I guess she doesn't care that the friction from her movement is nothing but enjoyment for me.

"Now, now, my little shortcake, calm down. Unless you want me to make a mess in my jeans."

She stops instantly, gasping as if appalled by my words. "You sick bastard. Are you really trying to get off right now?" She bucks her hips once more, causing me to groan.

I'm painfully hard, just as I always have been in her presence. "Don't act like you don't feel my hardness pressed against that soft flesh of yours, shortcake. You always loved this position, too." I lean over her, getting closer to her ear. "My dirty girl used to love letting me get off just . . . like . . . this." I roll my hips, letting my hardness press tightly against her ass and pussy.

Her breathing picks up, but she shuts it down just as quickly. "Yeah, well, that was a long fucking time ago. When I thought you gave a fuck about us. Not anymore, asshole. Now let me the fuck up!" She shoves back hard this time, causing me to lose my footing.

I let go so I can right myself.

"What do you want, Tank? Why am I really here?" She looks at me as if she hates me.

What the hell do I know? Maybe she does. She has to feel something similar to hate in order to keep my son away from me. "You're here because your son came to me and my club for help, for protection. He was afraid you were going to end up dead if he didn't do something soon. What's going on, Lay? Why the hell are you staying with this man if he beats on you and violates you? You and those boys deserve so much more than that."

She cocks her head to one side, looking at me as if I'm a complete stranger. "Are you serious right now, Zane? You have no right to tell me what my boys and I deserve. You fucking left us almost sixteen years ago, you bastard!" She starts hitting my chest with both fists as tears roll down her face.

She screams at me for leaving them, for all the pain they've endured since I've been gone, and for the fact that I never came back. She tells me repeatedly how much she hates me for the pain I've caused. It breaks my heart to see her this way, to know I've unintentionally hurt her this much. But as much as I want her forgiveness, I'm not sure she'll ever have mine. What she took from me . . . I can never get back.

LAYLA

I'm sweating. I never keep it this hot in my room. Slinging the cover off, I roll over to snuggle my other pillow, only it's not my pillow at all. It's a very hot, very hard body. I jump back, forgetting this is not my bed. It's a smaller bed I realize as I fall off and onto a hard-ass floor. "Motherfucker, that hurt." I grab the back of my head to make sure it isn't bleeding.

"Lay, are you okay?" a groggy voice says from beside me, scaring the fuck out of me once again.

I look up to see a huge, hard penis bouncing in front of me as a very naked Tank stands over me. I swallow hard, trying to get myself together. It's then I realize the majority of my clothes are gone as well. I'm in a thin tank top and panties which are extremely wet right now. Tank bends down to assess me. I can't speak because my damn mouth is so dry my tongue is stuck.

He flashes a knowing smile, the smug fucker.

"Shortcake, are you okay?"

I nod and say the first thing that comes to mind, "I'm thirsty."

He says nothing as he stands then walks across the room. I won't lie and say I'm not watching his tight, muscular ass as he bends down to a little mini-fridge and pulls out a soda then brings it to me. He does all of this while wearing the same smug look on his face. Bastard.

"Like what you see, shortcake? You can have a taste if you want it. I promise not to leave you thirsty."

My mouth has no problem whatsoever dropping open in shock. He winks at me and laughs all the way to what I'm assuming is the bathroom. My assumption is confirmed when I hear his piss hit the toilet while he's still laughing.

How the fuck did I get here? If someone would have told me yesterday I would wake up today in bed with my ex I wouldn't have believed that shit, but I would have at least shaved my hoo-ha. You know, just in case. I hurry back to the bed, making sure to cover all of my goodies before he gets back. Maybe if I play like I'm asleep he'll leave me alone.

"I know you're not asleep, Layla. I can hear your loud-ass breathing from way over here."

I should have known he wouldn't leave me be and take his ass back to sleep. I sit up, making sure to hold the cover tight to my body so nothing is given away. My slutty nipples perk up around him.

"What? Do you have something on your mind that you need to get off?" He smirks. "I definitely need to get off, but I'll take care of that later." He's silent for a few minutes, so his words are left hanging in the air.

I let them sink in and I know exactly what he means. He's not talking about getting off with me, but with one of the half-naked whores running around here. I will not let him know I'm affected by his words. I fucking refuse to.

"I'm sure there's something else you want to share other than your sexual escapades."

He stares at me with a look I wasn't expecting. It's one of sadness, one of grief. "Why did you name him Brady? Out of all the names we talked about if we ever had kids, Brady was not one of them. So, why did you name him that?"

His anger about this is pissing me off. I don't hold back as I jump up and stand directly in front of him, not caring one fucking bit that he's still naked as the day he was born. I'm tired of his bullshit. Raising my voice so loudly I'm sure this whole fucking clubhouse can hear me, I tell him about himself, "I named him Brady because he's part of you, you fucking prick. Your brother was your world up until the day he died."

He grabs my arm and jerks me around until my back hits the wall. "Don't stand here and talk about him! Don't you fucking dare, Layla."

Yanking my arm out of his hold, I yell louder, "Him? Fucking Him! Can you not even say his name, or call him your fucking brother? You act like you're ashamed of him or something, Zane! Why?"

His eyes are watery, but his anger shows through. "Get the fuck out of my room. It would be in your best interest to stay as far away from me as fucking possible during your stay here. I don't want to see your face."

I know he's upset, but his words still hurt. I refuse to show it though. I walk to the door aware that I'm only in panties and a thin tank top. I turn the knob and step out into the hallway, but I get in one last "fuck you" before slamming his door.

Quietly standing there, I listen as Tank's fists hit the door. He lets out a growl of pure anguish, along with a slew of cuss words. As soon as he gets quiet, I walk away not knowing where the hell I'm going to sleep tonight.

"Hey, girl, put these on." A large guy gives me a pair of women's sleep shorts.

"Um, thank you, but no thanks. I don't know where or who those came from. No offense, but I don't want to catch any type of STD from wearing anything that came off of the women I've seen here."

He smiles a genuine smile, almost a laugh, but I've seen enough pain in my life to know that a lot is hiding behind his beautiful eyes. "Don't worry, they don't belong to any of the sluts around here. They belong to Navy, and I know they're clean because I just got them from the dryer."

I'd met Navy earlier. "She's Memphis' ol' lady, right?"

He nods. "Yeah, she claims his ugly ass."

A throat clears as I'm taking the shorts out of his hand.

"Snoop got you out of your clothes already, Layla?" Navy says as she comes out of the hallway with her arm wrapped around Memphis' waist.

Snoop, as she calls him, laughs out loud. "She can only dream about this shit, Navy. I'm not trying to die at the hands of Tank over some cooch."

I scoff. "I beg your pardon, Snoopy, is it? It will be you doing the dreaming about this . . . cooch."

He laughs again and it changes his face. He has a beautiful smile. "I like you, Layla. See ya tomorrow."

* * *

He's now gone, leaving me with Navy and Memphis. Navy speaks first, "I'm sorry for the way Tank talked to you."

My face heats.

"Yeah, you can hear pretty much everything in here. I never knew Prez had a brother. He's never said anything, not one single word in all these years," Memphis says in a sad tone.

I shake my head. It hurts me to know he carries so much pain and guilt that he won't even speak about Brady. "The only reason I know about him is one year on Brady's birthday, Zane came home so drunk he could hardly walk. Thank God he got someone else to bring him home that night instead of taking his bike. He would have never made it had he decided to drive. I won't tell you what he told me had happened because it's not my story to tell, but just know that he loved Brady so very much.

"Their dad was never around, so Brady looked up to Zane for everything. Zane holds a lot of self-hate and guilt. He takes full responsibility for his brother's death. It ate him alive back then and the only thing that's changed is that he has tried to block out that whole part of his life like it never existed."

This is a family, they take care of one another; I can tell by the sadness and hurt on their faces. That being said, I wonder why he never told them about him, unless he really has blocked it all away and our son being named Brady is bringing back all the memories he's tried so hard to suppress all these years.

"Can I ask you a question about Brady, his brother?" Memphis asks.

I nod. "Of course, but I don't know that much about him other than what he spewed that night."

"Is his birthday March nineteenth?"

I open my mouth to ask how he knows if Zane has never spoken of him, but close it just as fast. I already know why he knows this date. "He still disappears and gets shit-faced on his birthday, doesn't he?"

They look at each other, then at me. "Every single year for as long as I can remember. We never pushed him about it, but could always tell when it was getting close because his whole demeanor changed for at least a couple of weeks prior."

"Damn, I wish he would have told us, so we could be there for him. We're a fucking family, that's what we do. It kinda hurts he don't trust us enough to let us in," Memphis says as he grabs Navy's hand, pulling her toward the hallway. "Come on, sis, you can sleep on the couch in our room until Mr. Grumpy Pants gets his head out of his ass." Memphis nods his head in the direction of their bedroom.

The couch is awesome, but I doubt I'll get sleep due to my thoughts wandering to the heartbroken asshole in the other room.

I wake up to the sight of chubby cheeks, wild eyes, and crazy, dark curls on one of the most beautiful little girls I've ever seen. I saw the same set of eyes yesterday, which means this little princess has to belong to Navy and Memphis.

"Hi, beautiful, what's your name?"

She giggles, turns, and wobbles away.

"Bella! Bella! Oh my gosh, Layla, I'm so sorry. Did she wake you?" Navy comes in and scoops her up and onto her right hip. "How many times has Mommy told you not to run away?"

She leans in and gives her mom a sloppy kiss on the cheek before giggling once again. I love it and miss the sound of a laughing child.

"Well, she definitely gets that from her dad. Every time I try to scold him about something, he does the same thing."

We both laugh, causing little Bella to laugh too.

"She's beautiful. I can tell she belongs to you guys. She's the perfect combination of you both."

Navy smiles as she takes in her little girl, then nods her head in agreement. "Thank you, I think so too. She takes her stubbornness from her dad though, because I am not stubborn at all." She says with a wink in my direction.

"Dammit, Navy, are you in here lying again? She will get to know you and see for herself just how stubborn you are. You do know that, right? Now, give me my damn princess." A biker with a bit of an accent and beautiful hair grabs Bella as if she were his own, cooing to her as he strolls away without a second glance.

I guess I look confused because Navy takes it upon herself to inform me, "That's my brother Capone. Not blood, but just as close if not closer. You'll get to know them all better the longer you're here, hon."

My son Brady walks up behind Navy, asking if he can have a minute with me before breakfast. She puts one hand on his cheek, giving him a peck on the other. "Absolutely, Brady. Don't forget to wash up." She leans in as if to whisper, but I know she's intentionally louder so I can hear her when she says, "Take it easy on her."

The reality is I am nowhere near prepared for this conversation. I honestly didn't think about him being angry at me, as well as his father. Shit. I feel like such a horrible mom for not thinking about the thoughts that must be racing through my poor boy's head. "Son, I'm so—"

He slams the door and throws both hands in the air, cutting me off. "Did I not deserve the truth, Mom? Did I not deserve to know that I look just like a man who's walking around this earth and not buried six fucking feet under? You told me he was dead—as in no longer here." He's pacing back and forth, anger more evident with every step. "Well, guess what, Mom? He's fucking here and I look just like the motherfucker!"

I grab him by his shirt with both fists closed tight around the fabric. "I get that you're angry and not thinking straight right now, but you will not talk to me like that, Brady. At the end of the day, I'm still your fucking mother. I raised you by my damn self with absolutely no help from anyone except your brother, so you will show me the respect I deserve. We can either talk this shit out like rational adults or not at all because I refuse to be in a screaming match with my own damn child.

"Now, what's it gonna be?"

He looks at me with eyes full of hate, jaw clenched tight, then turns and slams his fist through the wall. He storms out without another word.

As I move to chase after him, I hear, "Stop, Lay. Just let him cool off."

Tank's voice from right outside the door, startles me, making my blood boil.

"Fuck you, you bastard," I say as I take off down the hallway not giving a damn how childish my response was just now. They aren't the only ones who can act like assholes—I can be the biggest asshole of them all. I've been through too much lately. I will not get away from one hell just to be placed in another and be mistreated all over again.

TANK

A s I sit in church waiting for the brothers to arrive, I can't help but think of last night and how I acted so out of character. I never treat women that way, ever. I especially never wanted to treat Layla like that, but he is not a subject that's up for discussion. She didn't know that, so I should have handled it better than I did. She's always had a way of getting under my skin, that hasn't changed. I don't know how to forgive her or move forward and it's killing me. One thing is for fucking sure though, he will not disrespect his mother around me. Regardless of her secrets, she raised him the best she could and damn sure doesn't deserve to be mistreated by him or anyone else, including myself.

"Prez, you good?" Snoop asks. He's the first one in. The others file in not far behind him.

I nod. "Yeah, I'm good. I'm just ready to take this piece of shit down so we can get back to our lives."

I've got four sets of curious eyes aimed in my direction. It's like they're waiting for me to talk about my fucking feelings so they can say "and how do you feel about that?" I hate this shit, being looked at like I'm going to break or flip my shit.

"What the fuck are y'all looking at?" I yell, knocking my papers off the table.

But they never divert their eyes as I do exactly what they were waiting for me to do. Fuck this shit. "Does anyone have anything on the precinct yet? Have we heard anything from Tats, Dodger, or Scar? Please tell me they've caught them with their dicks in the dirt somewhere in that country-ass podunk town, please." I wait for someone to speak, but no one does, which pisses me off. "So, what's this shit about, huh? No one's gonna talk or spill any info until I go all sappy and start talking about my fucking feelings. Is that it? Well, it's not gonna fucking happen."

More silence, more concerned fucking faces and I'm about to lose my shit.

"I'm the fucking president of this club. I make the rules, I run this shit. So, someone better start talking right the fuck now!" I look around the table.

None of my brothers show fear because they know me, and even that makes me fucking angry. One thing in my life I can't talk about. One fucking thing they don't know and they're pressing me to talk about it. I won't, not this.

"Everybody, get out! Just get the fuck out and stay out of my way today. I'll get my own information. I don't need this shit." I walk out of the church, which is something I never do, and go search for my son.

It's time I let him know who I am and how we do shit around here. He needs to know that his smart-ass mouth won't fly here. He may not know me or like me, but he's about to learn a fucking lesson in respect.

* * *

"How could you do this to me, Johnny? I would've never kept anything like this from you. You never knew your fucking dad, so I'm not supposed to know mine either, is that it?"

I walk in on the end of the conversation, just as Brady shoves Johnny, then swings, connecting with his jaw. Johnny looks at his brother as if devastated that he raised his hand to him.

"That's fucking code, Johnny. We're brothers! Why? Fucking tell me!" Brady lunges at Johnny again, only this time, I catch him around his waist and push him backward.

"It's not his fucking fault that you didn't know about me. You wanna hit someone? Grab a set of fucking gloves and a headpiece and meet me in the basement."

He looks at me like I'm crazy, as does everyone else not minding their own fucking business today.

"*Do it*! *Now!*" I walk away, trying to keep my cool as everyone continues to stare in my direction.

In our basement—not the side we take our enemies to meet their maker, but to the other side of the compound— we have a workout area, as well as a huge octagon ring. We use it to make a point or to get out some of our built-up rage when sex isn't doing the job.

"Why am I down here, old man, huh? What? You gonna beat on me too? You just like that bastard back home that beats my momma first, then me and Johnny? Is that what this is? Because if it is, I'm not holding back anymore. I held back with him because of her, but having your mama lie and tell you that your daddy is dead, only to have him walk into our house ten years later, very much alive, shows me that she never gave a fuck about my feelings. So I shouldn't give a damn about hers."

I'm shocked and angry. I can't believe Layla hated me so much that she would go as far as to tell my own flesh and blood I was dead. I'll deal with my feelings later, right now he needs to get all of that anger out.

I swing, hitting his headpiece hard, but not too hard. He growls in anger as he comes at me swinging. Surprisingly, I see that Johnny has shown him a few things I used to show him as a child because he goes straight for the body, catching me off guard.

As I let him take out his anger on me, I see his eyes well with tears. A crowd of brothers, members, Navy, and Layla are now watching from right outside the octagon. Layla has a hand over her mouth to cover up her sobs, and Navy comforts her with an arm around her shoulder.

I can tell my son is getting tired, but he won't give up. He screams at me, breaking what's left of my heart.

"Hit me, hit me, dammit! That's all I'm good for, isn't it? Just a fucking punching bag. My mama lied to me. My dad didn't want me. The only male figure I had other than Johnny hated me so much he beat me, broke my bones, and locked me in the fucking cellar with no food or water for fucking days. So, hit me, old man. I'm used to it." He sobs as he swings one last time and falls into my arms.

I see Layla start to run up, but Johnny grabs her, shaking his head. I'm grateful for that because this is my time. I hug my son so tight as I fall to my knees, pulling him into me. "I'm so sorry, son. If I had known about you I would have been a part of your life regardless of mine and your mom's status. Hear me good when I say that nothing or no one would have kept me from knowing or loving you. You look exactly like me, son. Bull-headed just the same too." I feel a small shake as though that comment made him chuckle, so I pull him back to see his face.

He still looks as if he's truly devastated by the latest events happening in his life. I can't blame him, it's a fucked up situation. This shit is gonna take a while to recover from, especially for him.

"I'm gonna kill that bastard for ever thinking he could put his hands on my sons. I'm so sorry you and Johnny had to suffer through so much, but I can promise you now that it will never happen again. Got me?"

He nods with a small, but sad smile. "Yeah, old man, I got you."

I tap my glove on the side of his head. "I got your old man, you little shit."

We both get to our feet, but stop as we realize the whole room is full, all eyes on us.

"Damn, can me and my son not have a moment without y'all acting like some damn girls?" I wrap my arm around his shoulder. "Since everyone is already here tonight, we celebrate. We celebrate my two boys coming home to stay."

I look right at Layla, letting her see that I won't let them go. I see fire in her tear-filled eyes. She knows if she leaves, my boys won't be with her this time around.

The room erupts with clapping and laughter as everyone makes their way out, but Layla stops me.

"Go on, son. Go with the brothers and tell them all your favorite foods, so we can get everything together." He nods and as soon as he's out of sight I lose my shit on her, "How could you allow our kids to be beaten and locked in a fucking cellar with no fucking food, Layla? What the hell were you doing while they were starving, huh? Dammit! I can't even look at you the same anymore. It makes me fucking sick!" I move to walk away from her but her voice cracks, stopping me.

She tries to speak but fails. Her body shudders with sobs as she runs out of the basement. How could she let my kids suffer like that without reaching out to me?

"She didn't know, asshole. We didn't tell her everything he did because we didn't want her to fight him and end up fucking dead."

"Johnny, this shit is hard for me to understand, son. Your mom was always a strong woman in every way that counts, so excuse me if I don't understand how she let this shit happen."

He shakes his head. "Like I said, old man, we didn't tell her everything. The more she fought him, the more he hurt her, so we learned not to tell her how bad things got while he had her tied down or locked up somewhere. You need to know all the details before you just start talking shit to her, causing her more pain."

I guess I need to sit down and talk to Layla about this shit without getting angry. In my heart, I know she would never have allowed any of it to happen. I'm just having a hard time understanding why she never reached out to me for help.

* * *

I can hear her crying as I stand outside Memphis' door, trying to figure out what I'm going to say to her. I hate that she's hurting, but so are we. Maybe I can be more sensitive, caring to her sadness, once I understand why she never told me or reached out. That, to me, is unacceptable.

LAYLA

I hear the door creak as it's slowly pushed open. I know exactly who it is, I can smell him from here. He's always used the same body wash—birchwood, sweet and clean with that minty touch that I love. "Please leave, Tank. I'm not in the mood to be told, once again, what a horrible mother I've been to my kids." I hear his boots hit the floor, coming in my direction, ignoring my request as usual.

"Our," is all he says.

It's enough to get me off the couch and in his face. "*Our*! *Our*? Really, Zane?" I yell, shoving my finger into his chest. "No, not ours, you asshole. Mine! You don't get to come back into our lives after fifteen plus years when I've already raised *my* sons and try to play daddy now! Maybe all of the drugs and alcohol over the years have ruined what was left of your brain cells because that's not how shit works."

He smirks before walking toward me. It's not one of

his sexy smirks, either. Oh, no, it's pure evil. "Well, let me just start off with the fact that you know I don't do drugs—alcohol, yes, but never drugs. Secondly, I'm no doctor, but I'm pretty sure me coming so many times inside your pussy bare is what led to our son being here. That means he's got my blood running through his veins, too. I wouldn't have to come back almost sixteen years later had you not pushed me away in the fucking first place when all I wanted to do was protect you, Johnny, and him—had I known there was a fucking *him*!"

He's really going to stand here and act like I didn't send letter after letter for almost six fucking years letting him know about Brady, asking him to please come get us. Fuck him. I refuse to let him play this shit on me. "If he's so much your son, let me hear you say his fucking name. I haven't heard you call him by his name since you found out about him. It's either *him*, *his*, *son*, or *boy*. You can't even call him by his motherfucking name, Zane. I make you sick? No, motherfucker. *You* make *me* sick. He's your fucking son, who's named after your only brother, and you refuse to call him by his damn name because your brother is no longer here and you blame yourself! Get over yourself, asshole!"

He's livid. I can practically feel the anger vibrating off of him. "If you know what's good for you, bitch, you'll never talk to me like that again. Never bring him up. Fucking ever!"

So much for explaining that this was the first I've heard of my kids going without food or having any broken bones. I would have killed the son of a bitch myself if I'd known. There's no way he'll listen now that I've pissed him off bad enough for him to call me a bitch. He's only done that one other time: The day I told him he wasn't welcome to come back.

* * *

The boys' celebration turned out really nice, if you exclude the half-naked whores walking around the room, grinding on the members, including Tank. I know I mean nothing to him anymore but a part of me will always love him, so seeing other women grinding on his lap fucking pisses me off.

"Looks like Prez is gonna need a little push, beautiful." I turn around and see the same man who gave me the shorts when Tank kicked me out of his room practically naked. I believe his name is Snoopy.

Before I can ask what he means, his mouth slams over mine. He slides his tongue inside, causing me to moan, loud.

He chuckles. "Easy, baby girl. We want him angry not fucking murderous." He laughs before grabbing my ass and taking my lips once more.

I could almost get lost in his kiss. It's been so long since someone has kissed me like this and not forced themselves on me, but the sounds of things being broken in the background distract me.

Snoopy pulls back and smiles the sweetest smile. "That should do the trick, princess, but do me a favor and stay out of what happens next. Okay?"

I'm confused until I see Tank running in our direction, ramming his shoulder into Snoop's stomach.

"Oh my God! Stop it, Tank, before you hurt him." I go to grab Tank's arm, but Snoopy yells at me.

"It's okay, beautiful. Remember what I said."

That pisses Tank off more, causing him to throw punch after punch into Snoop's body. "Don't you fucking call her that or put your mouth on her body, you piece of fucking shit." Tank swings hard, hitting him in the left eye.

"That all you got, pussy? Yeah, that's right, only pussy-ass boys call beautiful women like Layla bitches."

Tank lets out a noise that sounds anything but human as he picks him up by his shirt. "You don't know shit about having a woman and kid you can't see. You don't know what the fuck I've gone through. You putting your mouth on my fucking ol' lady is something that calls for punishment like no other, motherfucker."

Snoop laughs before spitting blood onto the floor. "Punish me all you fucking want, old man. My mission is accomplished."

Something flashes in Tank's eyes as Snoop's words register. I'm assuming he came to the same conclusion I did: Snoop was trying to help him open his eyes to what's right in front of him.

Tank puts him down and turns to look at me, but before he speaks Snoop grabs his shoulder to turn him around.

The whole room is quiet as Snoop says his piece, "You don't know me either, asshole. At least your kid is here, alive. Your baby mama is right here, right in front of you and you are treating her like shit. Yeah, she was fucking wrong for not telling you about your son, but at the end of the day, Tank, they're right fucking here. Alina and my son are both gone.

"Her parents didn't like the fact that their daughter was seeing an older boy, especially one from the dirty trailer park across town. When they found out she was pregnant her dad went ape shit and made her get rid of my fucking son. After that, no matter how much I fucking loved her, I couldn't get past that shit, so she enlisted with my sister Asia. I haven't spoken to her since.

"So, again, bro, at least they're here."

My heart hurts for Snoop as I watch him walk away with so much sadness weighing on him.

Tank grabs my hand and drags me down the hall to his room. As soon as the door shuts he's on me. His rough hands on my thighs as he lifts me up, putting my legs around his waist. "I'm sorry, Layla, so fucking sorry for calling you a bitch." He kisses me and it's like no time has passed since his lips were on mine. I love the way he nibbles and bites at my lips before kissing them so sweetly. He lays me on the bed and slides in between my open thighs. "I won't say I'm not angry anymore, but I want to understand your side and why all of these things happened. I need to know why you never reached out to me, but right now, at this moment, I just need you. I need to be close to you, inside of this beautiful body I have missed for so many years.

"Do you want that? If you don't, I need you to tell me now because I will never do anything to you that's not wanted, ever."

I turn my head, ashamed of the things I know my boys have probably told him.

"Don't do that, shortcake. You have nothing to be

ashamed of. That bastard took from you, and he is the one who should be ashamed, baby. Not you, never you." He kisses me softly and begins to pull away but my legs wrap around his waist.

"No, please don't go, Zane."

He makes this sexy sound in the back of his throat before settling back in between my legs. I can feel the hardness pushing through his jeans against the cloth of my panties.

"Damn, shortcake, I can feel your heat through my jeans. I've missed these legs, so silky soft." He slides down, slowly pushing my dress up over my navel before placing a soft, wet kiss beside it.

Once those rough hands reach my hips, I'm panting. There's something to be said about calloused hands on smooth, soft skin. He places a kiss on my wet panties before pulling them down my legs, leaving me bare. The cool air from the window blows through, making me shiver as it hits the wetness of my lips and clit.

"Look at my sweet girl, shaking and needy. This is a sight I thought I'd never get to see again," he says, staring between my open legs.

"And you won't ever get to again if you don't move."

He looks up at me as he leans back to remove his kut and shirt, then stands to remove his boots and jeans.

I know he's purposely taking his time. He knows I'm a very impatient woman, which is why I slide my hand down between my legs and begin circling my clit with my fingers. He stops me, grabbing my hand and sliding the two fingers I was using into his mouth, sucking them slowly, enjoying the taste.

"Mm, babe, you have no idea how much I miss this taste, your smell, every fucking thing about this body." He slams both of my hands down beside my thighs as he buries his face in my pussy. My ass comes up off the bed, pushing my wetness further into his face. He lets go of my hands so he can wrap his arms around my thighs and hold me down.

Not being able to move makes the feeling so much more intense as he bites and licks at my swollen clit. "Ah, please, please, Zane!"

He sucks at my clit harder, making me feel things I haven't felt in so many years. My body feels like it's going to explode from so much pleasure.

"Please what, shortcake? Tell me what you need."

I pull my dress the rest of the way off then snap my bra off as well. As soon as the air hits my already-hard nipples, I moan louder. "Fuck yes! I need to come, Zane, please, baby."

He licks, bites, and sucks my needy clit until I'm about to come. I feel it and I know he can feel it too because he slows down and licks his way up my stomach until he reaches my breast. He sucks my left nipple into his mouth, teasing me before making his way over to my right nipple, which for some reason is more sensitive than my left. He bites down hard as he slams his cock inside of me.

I come instantly.

"Yes! Fuck yes, baby girl, that's it. Come all over my cock." He plays every sweet spot on my body as he pounds into my pussy with a hard, swollen cock.

It seems bigger than I remember, if that's even possible. He's always been above average in that department.

"You're drenched, baby; so fucking wet for me. I'm about to make you so much wetter. Fuck . . . yes . . . Ugh, ugh." He pinches my clit as he comes inside of me, causing me to come again.

My body is up off the bed, my ass cheeks clutched in his hands as he bites my nipple. We both come, hard.

I feel boneless and sated as my back hits the mattress and my eyes close. "Mm, yes, thank you, Zane."

His laughing is the last thing I hear before falling asleep.

TANK

I heard from Dane this morning, so I'm in a grand-ass mood as I walk into church. The best sex of my life might have played a part in my mood as well. Scratch that shit—I *was* in a good mood, until I see the shit-eating grins on every brothers' face. Even with Snoop sporting a black eye, he's still smiling ear to ear. Smug bastard.

"I don't know why all of you assholes are smiling, especially you, dickhead." I point to Snoop. "Your punishment will be determined today, and you should know, it's not gonna be an easy one."

His smile never fades as he continues to look me in the eyes. "I'm sure whatever you dish out, old man, I can take. After last night, I doubt you have any strength left anyway, so it can't be that bad."

He's baiting me, trying to piss me off, and it's working. "I handled your big ass just fine from the look of your face, asshole."

He smirks, making his busted lip more noticeable. "It's not my ass I was thinking of when I said you'd have no energy left, old man. I think I can speak for the whole clubhouse when I say that we heard you handle ass in a different way last night, but if it makes you feel any better it sounded like you really beat that shit up, Prez."

I'm across the table, him pulled up out of his chair before the other brothers get me off of him. "Don't you dare talk about her that way, Finn, fucking ever. I will kill your ass, brother or not. You crossed a fucking line last night when you put your hands and dirty-ass mouth on my property and, had it not been for my son watching, there would have been more damage."

The motherfucker laughs in my face, causing the whole room to cackle like a bunch of old-ass broads at a bingo session. I jerk my arms out of Capone's and Memphis' grasps.

"Let me go before both of you assholes end up on the same level as this fucking imbecile."

They don't give a fuck as they shake in laughter all the way back to their seats.

"Hey, I'm not stupid. Very clever, actually, seeing as my plan worked out perfectly. We all know Layla is your one regret; it was evident on your face when you laid eyes on her again. You were acting like a jackass though. Allowing your anger to cloud your judgment when it came to her. I just helped you clear the air." He shrugs his shoulders as if he's proud of himself.

"Enough of this bullshit, let's get down to business.

Tats, Dodge, and Scar have been up there for a couple of days now but said Byron hasn't even so much as pulled in the driveway of their home. I find that shit a little suspicious myself. I'm certain we didn't have a tail on our way back with them and all of their phones were thrown out not far from their house, so there's no way to trace them back here. Any ideas on what in the actual fuck is going on?"

All laughter is gone now, as this is a very serious matter. This motherfucker is dangerous and off of our radar, which is never a good thing. We need eyes on the enemy at all times, but being as he doesn't have any way to connect Layla to me, there's no way he's a threat right now.

"Dane said he's been in touch with an officer in that precinct on Byron's payroll, trying to find a way off of it without becoming another body with a toe tag. Apparently, this guy knows a lot more than Byron knows he knows, and he's on his way to meet up with our boy Dane right now.

"This may be the break we need, so I told the boys to head on back. No need to waste time. If he was gonna show his face he would have done it by now. Plus, Tats is getting a little homesick and misses being able to have ass on tap—his words not mine. He said the bitches down there are country as fuck and mean as striped snakes."

We all laugh because Tats is a big-ass dude, so for him to say that bitches are mean is just downright hilarious.

"I guess we just stay close and wait to hear from Dane. Until then, I'm gonna go find my kid and see how much he hates me."

They all get up, except for Snoop. "We good or what, Prez?"

I stare at him to make him shake a bit. "We're good. I know your heart was in the right place and you were only trying to help me, which I appreciate, but never touch my woman again, Snoopy. You got me?"

He nods while smiling as he makes his way to the door. "Oh, Snoop."

He turns.

"I'm sorry to hear about your baby and your girl. That's a fucked up situation. I'm sure it's not an easy thing to have dealt with alone. We are your brothers and you can always talk to us about anything, remember that."

He nods once more. "Yeah, Prez, you remember that, too, when March nineteenth rolls around."

I don't know how much time has passed since Snoop's last comment was made, but it knocked me back into a deep, dark part of my past.

TANK

Age Eighteen

"**C**ome on, Zane, just let me ride with you guys tonight. She's drunk as usual and won't even know I'm gone," Brady begs.

"I said no for the hundredth time, Brady. This isn't a place you need to be, man. You're still a kid. I don't want my kid brother getting into any trouble." I love my brother, but he doesn't understand how dangerous it is running with this crew. We do bad things that I don't want him involved in. He's better than this, better than me. His heart is so big and he's always looking up to me when that's the last thing he should do.

I'm a fucking reckless-ass mess—alcohol, drugs, gang banging, you name it, I do it. I feel like my life is already shit, but Brady is smart and he can go places. That's why I do a lot of the shit I do, so he can have the better things in life since our sorry-ass mom won't be providing it for him. If it's not a Xanax or some sort of pain pill, she doesn't give a fuck. I'll make sure Brady makes it though.

I've been saving after every transaction is done, so he can go to college and get the fuck out of this city. Some people are made for these city streets, but not my little brother.

TANK

"**T**ank? Tank, are you okay?"

I look up to see a concerned Layla standing in front of me, but my focus is thrown off when I realize she's wearing my black, sleeveless Guardian Angels T-shirt. If my eyes are not deceiving me, and I pray they are not, it's the only thing she has on.

I get up and lock the door then go back to sit in my desk chair. "On the table now, spread em wide."

Her eyes go as wide as saucers, but she complies, doing exactly as she's told. I was right in thinking my shirt was all she had on, because on my desk, with her legs spread wide, she bares to me a very wet cunt.

I slide my chair closer, so I can indulge this sweet little pussy. "You smell exactly like I remember." I take a long, slow lick, making her squirm. "I remember coming home from work and being able to smell your needy pussy as soon as I opened our bedroom door. You laid on the bed, waiting for me. Your beautiful bare pussy on display just for me." Another lick, then another, before sucking her swollen clit into my mouth. I love the way her body responds to me— she arches into my mouth, feeding me as she grinds slowly on my tongue and lips.

"Yes, oh yes. I always wanted to please you when you came home from a hard day's work. I . . . ah, I wanted to show you how much I missed you while you were gone. How much my body missed you being inside of it. Mm . . . please, Zane, don't stop."

I flick the tip of my tongue quickly across her little bundle of nerves, causing her to buck her hips. I kick the chair back and pull her up onto her knees, so I can place my head under her body. "Sit that pretty pussy on my face, shortcake."

She does exactly that, riding my tongue like she's at the fucking rodeo, and fuck me, it's sexy as fuck.

"Oh, fuck, Zane baby. Fuck, fuck, please." She's twisting her sweet pussy all over my face as she begs.

I can't take it anymore. I'm hard as a rock, so this is guaranteed to be fast and hard. I pull her down from her knees and bend her over the table with nothing but that beautiful ass and pussy on display. "Baby, I'll make it up to you later, but this is gonna be fast."

She moans in response, and I grab a handful of her hair then slam inside.

As soon as I'm in her, I feel her muscles contract, squeezing the life out of my cock. "Fuck, baby, that feels good, so good."

I hear a hard knock on the door.

"Prez, you in there?"

I start to pull out, but Layla tightens her muscles again. I look up to see her head thrown back, mouth open, and eyes closed. She looks completely blissed out and sexy as fuck.

"Prez!" Capone yells.

"Go . . . *ugh* . . . the fuck . . . *ugh* . . . away." I keep pounding into her as she reaches down between her legs. I can feel her rubbing her clit, as well as my shaft, which shoots me over the fucking edge.

She slams back against me as I slam in—that's all it took for us both. I'm biting down hard, trying to keep quiet, and taste blood. Layla, apparently, doesn't care who hears her as she screams out my name.

"You gonna fall asleep on me again, pretty girl?"

She huffs out a laugh. "I don't have any idea what you're talking about." She laughs again as she tries to fix her hair before walking over to unlock and open the door.

Capone's hand hovers, about to knock again.

"Dammit, pretty boy, can't a girl get laid in fucking privacy? I mean, really? Do you know how long it's been since I've gotten laid properly and was able to get off too?"

Capone's eyes widen at Layla's outburst. He looks to me with a *what the fuck* look, but all I can do is laugh. That's the Layla I remember. The girl who wasn't afraid to speak her mind and didn't take shit from anyone. I need to find out what happened to that Layla.

"Look, I'm sorry to interrupt, Tank, but Dane is here and he's got that cop from North Georgia with him."

I'm already moving toward the door. "Why the hell

didn't you say that to begin with, dumbass?"

He's right on my heels as we make our way to the main bar area. "Probably because I had to wait until your ol' lady got off properly before y'all would open the damn door, dipshit."

We all have a drink at the bar before making our way into the church. I've got the feeling that this will be one long-ass meeting.

"Damn, it smells like pussy in here," Tats says. " No, fuck that. It smells like someone had one hell of a fuck fest in this room."

All eyes turn to me.

"Shut the fuck up, Snoopy."

Capone is the first one to laugh, causing everyone to follow.

LAYA

"**S**o, what? Now you and my sperm donor are a thing again? I hope you are at least using fucking birth control this time, Layla. I would hate for another kid to grow up without a father because you refused to tell him the truth. I can't believe you, Mom. You just got out of one shit relationship to what? Jump in the bed with the President of an MC? A man who has more ass running around for him than he can probably handle. Come on, Mom, you are way smarter than this." He hit his target—he wanted to hurt me and he succeeded, but I'm still his mom and will not allow him to continue talking to me like this.

"You listen to me and you better listen good, because I won't have this conversation with you again. I am your mother and I love you more than you will ever understand unless you decide to have your own children. Then, and only then, will you understand what lengths you'll go to make sure your kids don't suffer any pain.

"Now, with that being said, I did reach out to your father for almost six years with not one response. I sent letter after letter, son. I wanted you to know Zane and I wanted him to know the amazing little boy we created together, out of love. I loved your father then and I will always love him even though I will never understand why he never came for us.

"I know that we went our separate ways before I found out about the pregnancy, but I was so sure that once he found out about you he would come back for us. We are supposed to have a long conversation tonight to clear up all of the confusion. He acts as if he never knew about you, but I know for a fact I mailed numerous letters in hopes he would come. On your fifth birthday, when you asked me about your dad, I couldn't hurt you. I didn't want to tell my beautiful little boy that every time I reached out I received nothing in return. I made a choice that day. I see now it was the wrong choice and I'm so sorry for not being honest back then. I love you, Brady."

He has tears in his eyes when I kiss his cheek and leave him to let everything sink in. I need to talk to Zane right now. Something just isn't adding up. Church or not, I need answers now.

TANK

"**W**ait, wait, so you're Mike, the cop I talked to all those years ago about Layla and Johnny?"

The guy sitting in front of me is shaking in his boots and has every reason to be scared shitless—I'm pissed, as is every brother in this room.

"Yes, I wanted to continue helping by keeping an eye on them for you, but Jamison is a mean son of a bitch and once he found out I was giving you intel, he lost his shit. He said he was going to kill my daughter if I gave you anything else on them. He showed me pictures of her at college, letting me know he's got someone on her in case I fuck up. I wanted to tell you about your son. I even tried to get one of the letters to you before he intercepted it, but he caught me getting it and questioned my loyalty. I lied, of course, saying I was just getting it for him.

"I don't know what you did to him, but he hates you, Tank. He's the type of guy you try to stay on good terms with because the alternative is death and you'll never see him coming before he strikes. He likes the element of surprise. A perfectly executed surprise takeover is what gets him off. He's a sick, twisted bastard."

I'm in shock at the shitload of information he's just dropped on us. Everyone in this room looks ready to murder this piece of shit. "He's the reason you got a new phone and fell off the map, huh?"

He nods.

What I'm confused about is how this motherfucker knows me. Hell, I never even knew his name until Johnny showed up on my doorstep. "Shit just ain't adding up."

* * *

The door flies open and standing there is a very upset Layla. "You can say that shit again." She's as beautiful as ever, her hair up in a messy bun with absolutely no makeup on and pissed, with both hands on her hips. "I just had a heartbreaking conversation with my child, and while explaining to him how many times I reached out to you, only to be ignored, something dawned on me. We've been so busy we haven't discussed why the fuck you are acting like I never told you about Brady. I sent so many letters that—" she stops speaking as she notices the officer sitting at the table.

She lunges at him. "You—you bastard, you could have helped me and my kids. You just stood there and watched him fucking beat me! I silently begged you for help every time he punched me in the fucking face." She clamps her hands around his neck.

Every brother in the room rises from their seats to stop her. I hold my hand up, letting them know not to touch her. "Let it play out. She needs this." They all sit back down and like myself, enjoy the show.

My girl is feisty for sure.

"Why didn't you help me?" she screams at him.

His face is turning red as tears roll down his cheek. For some reason, my gut tells me it's not because he's in pain or short of breath. It's because of his guilt.

"Stop, Layla!" I yell.

She doesn't let go. "No, Zane. This asshole could have helped me escape my hell had he just told the right people what he witnessed throughout the years. One word to the right person and my kids wouldn't have suffered. While I was tied up, raped, and beaten, my sons were hungry and thirsty in a fucking cellar. I had no idea while I laid there for days, wondering why they didn't help me."

I notice her grip isn't tight as I pull her hands away from him and take her into my arms.

"Layla, I'm so sorry. Please believe I tried, but that entire precinct is nothing if not corrupt." He stands, lifting his shirt, showing us severe scarring around his abdominal area. "This is the result of going to my captain about Byron Jamison. That was the day I found out just how far his reach was. He threatened my child's life if I didn't go along with his wishes." His head drops in what I can only describe as shame. "As much as I wanted to protect you and your boys

I had to make sure my daughter was protected as well. I did small things I'm sure you wouldn't have noticed—I made sure to volunteer as much as I possibly could without being noticeable, to be your watch. When I was there, at least I knew you weren't going to be harmed like I'm sure you were when he had Donavan on watch. I even tried to get one of your letters to Tank before he intercepted it, but he caught me."

Layla's mouth is open, eyes wide and angry.

"He's telling the truth, Mom." Our heads swing to the door as Johnny walks in. "I overheard Byron one day talking about how he thought Mike's loyalty was with you and your bastard kids instead of him. Whomever he was talking to he made it very clear that if things didn't change Officer Mike and his pretty little girl were to disappear for good. I had no idea who he was talking about then, but now, after hearing that, it adds up."

I should be a little upset with all the interruptions, as no one is supposed to step foot in this room during church other than members, but it seems we are getting to the bottom of things real quick. One thing I know for sure is that no one at that precinct will survive the hell that's coming their way. "So, they like the element of surprise, huh? Well, we're going to give them a fucking surprise." I sit back, tell Layla to go wait in my room, and then think of how to master my plan.

Johnny picks a chair to put his ass in and then I listen to all of the ideas being thrown out across the table. Capone, of course, wants to blow shit up. Memphis is more of a straight execution type of guy, whereas Snoopy, Crow, and Tats like it bloody. They like to drag out and torture the enemy, which in this situation, I'm thinking could be fun. Everyone else can go quickly, but Jamison will go nice and slow. He's hurt my woman and my kids. Unacceptable. He has no idea what the hell he's just brought to his door.

I'm a Guardian Angel through and through, but you fuck with my family and I'm coming in like the reaper to take your fucking soul.

"So, you never received any of the letters I wrote you about our son because that bastard intervened, as usual. I should have known he would do everything in his power to make sure you stayed away from us," Layla states quietly as if trying to wrap her head around everything that has happened.

I pull her into a tight embrace, letting her know we will figure this shit out together as a family. "That bastard will pay, shortcake. I promise you that."

She's crying into my shoulder, totally wrecked about this shit. I motion for the fellas to leave the room, so I can calm her down and clear a few things up.

"How, Zane? Tell me how I was with a man for over twelve years and never really knew him. He was so kind to me and my kids for the first few years of our relationship. Everything changed the day I brought up that you were Brady's father." She pulls away to take a seat.

I follow, taking the seat next to her. "I'm sorry, Layla, but I'm confused as to how this man knows me. I've never so much as seen this man's face."

She shakes her head. "That's the part I don't understand myself. A lot about this is confusing. I sent letters to you about Brady before he came into my life, or so I thought. It looks like maybe he was lurking in the shadows way before we got together. That's the only thing that makes any sense right now. My only question is why?"

That's exactly what I want to know myself.

"I saw little pieces of anger here and there, but after the conversation about you, the verbal abuse started and quickly escalated into physical abuse and threats. I never knew he hurt my kids that way. It kills me to know they suffered right along with me. I wanted to leave. I tried to leave, but he always threatened to kill my boys, and you. I couldn't let him kill my kids, Zane, or you." She breaks down again. "I called the police on him after the first time he put his hands on me only to have him show back up and beat me again for calling them. Johnny intervened a few times over the years, but it only made things worse. He had him arrested for a few different things that didn't set too well with the colleges he had applied to. He ruined my baby's chance at getting the fuck out of that town."

I can't wait to get my hands on this motherfucker. The more she talks the angrier I become.

My phone rings, making her jump. "It's okay, baby, it's just Tats calling." I press the phone to my ear. "Yeah, man, where the hell—wait, what?" I jump up and haul ass toward the door.

Layla is hot on my heels.

"Load up, we'll need the cage too. They fucking ambushed Tats, Scar, and Dodger." I turn to a scared-looking Layla. "Baby, I need you and the boys in the basement where the gym is. Crow and a few members will be here with you, as well as Dane and Mike. I'll be back soon." I give her a quick kiss before we're out the door and on our way.

I don't know how bad things are right now, but I do know it's gotta be pretty fucking bad for Tats to sound the way he did. They always take the backroads when coming home in case anyone tries to follow them back. It takes us about twenty-five minutes to get there. Absolutely nothing could have prepared me for the scene I pulled up on, nothing.

About a hundred feet of road is decorated with the blood and chunks of the flesh of my men. This much blood always brings back bad memories for me. I'm sure the end result will bring back the nightmares I try so hard to push away.

"Tats, Scar, Dodge!" we yell as we search the area.

I only see two bikes down, which means one is either missing or went off the embankment.

"Over here, brother," Tats yells as he struggles to get up the embankment.

We run to him and Memphis catches him right before he hits the ground. "Damn, how many times did you get hit, bro?" Memphis asks him frantically.

I hear the response but can't turn my head away from the ghastly sight in front of me. It's obvious that Tats and Scar were both shot from long range by a couple of rookies, thankfully.

Dodger didn't share the same fate.

"What the fuck happened? Why the fuck is his head—" I stop, not able to finish my sentence. I'll find out more once we get them home.

We load 'em into the cage, leaving some of the boys to clean up and get rid of the bikes.

"I can't fucking believe this, Prez. I tried to get his attention as soon as I saw the cable—I screamed his name—but he was too far ahead of us to hear me. He never saw it fucking coming. Fuck!" Tats screams out, his anguish palpable. If he's anything like me, this guilt, or whatever he's feeling, will be with him for a long time, if not forever.

Scar is quiet, looking as though he may be in shock.

"You okay, Scar? How many times were you hit?"

He nods, telling me, "Once."

"You know you can let go of his body, Scar. He's gone, brother."

He shakes his head, letting a tear fall. "He was so fucking excited about the possibility coming up for him to be patched in. It's my fault. It should have been me, not him. He's just a fucking kid. A fucking kid, Tank!" Tats is in pain, and beating himself up is not the answer right now, but I know trying to tell him that now won't go over too well.

We all sit in silence until we back the cage in around to unload Dodger's body. Memphis has already reached out to his sister to take care of the gunshot wounds. We lay Dodger's body onto a gurney we keep downstairs for situations like this. I slide the gurney with his body into the cooler until I break the news to Crow. This is going to crush him as Dodge was a good friend of his. They even started prospecting together, so this shit is gonna be hard. I leave Olivia with Tats and Scar, letting them know I need everyone in the church as soon as she's done.

The moment I walk into the gym, Layla, the boys, and Crow rush me. Dane and Mike follow shortly after.

"Zane, is everything okay? Are you hurt?" Layla is

looking me over, inspecting me, trying to see where all the blood is coming from.

I'm looking right at Crow. "It's not my blood, shortcake."

Crow looks at me, giving me a confused look.

I give Layla a short kiss, and my boys a quick pat on the shoulder. "I need all the boys in church in thirty minutes. I need to get a quick shower beforehand." I tell Dane and Mike that they need to be in church as well before I turn to leave.

Crow wasn't satisfied with what I had to say. "Don't do that shit, Tank. I'm a grown-ass man and a patched member of this club. I deserve to know what the fuck is going on."

I look him in the eyes because he's right and the fact he's not afraid to call me on my shit makes me proud to have him on our team. "I don't know all of the details just yet. I wanted to wait until we were all together to get those details, but what I can tell you is that both Scar and Tats have been shot, nothing fatal. I'm sorry, brother, but Dodger is gone."

A few different emotions cross his face—he goes from sad to angry quickly. "I'll see you in thirty minutes, Prez."

* * *

"Okay, okay. Everybody settle the fuck down. I want details. These sons of bitches are going to pay for our brother in that fucking cooler downstairs. Now, who wants to tell me what the fuck happened?"

Scar seems to be very distant right now, so Tats speaks up, "We were on Seventy-Five and decided to take the backroads the rest of the way. We rode for about ten miles when Dodger took the lead, enjoying the fucking weather. Scar was beside me, laughing as Dodge sped past us. When I looked back at him, I noticed a cable shoot up. I screamed his name, but he was too far ahead to hear me. That's when I felt the first shot hit my shoulder. The second came shortly after, knocking me off my bike. At the same time, Scar was hit and knocked off of his. I stood just in time to see two black SUVs with blacked-out windows pull out of the woods on each side of the road heading my way."

Crow is out of his seat, pacing the room. "So, you're saying that my fucking friend, my brother, was fucking decapitated by a motherfucking cable. Is that what I'm hearing right now?" He bends down to look Tats in the eyes. "Is that what happened to my brother, man? Is he really laying down there in a freezer with his head disconnected from his fucking body? Tell me that's not true, Tats. Tell me!" He slams his fist on the table.

Scar puts his hand on Crow's shoulder. "I'm sorry, brother, but it's true."

LAYLA

It's been a little over a month since we laid Dodger to rest. Things around here are finally getting back to normal. Well, as normal as they can be, considering everything that's gone on in the past couple of months.

Byron hasn't been heard from or seen since the ambush, and even then, he was never seen. But we all know he is responsible. Tonight, we celebrate the life of Dodger. We had to wait until Tats' and Scar's wounds healed before having the party Dodger would have wanted.

Crow is having one hell of a time accepting the death of his brother. He's been distant and somewhat angry, which is understandable in this situation. Everybody is angry that Byron is nowhere to be found, leaving them unable to get the revenge they are all wanting so badly, including me.

"You look good, Mama. Who are you trying to impress?"

I turn to see Johnny and Brady standing at the door.

"Thank you, baby. You boys look good too. Who are you trying to impress, hmm?" I cock my head to the side, making them both laugh.

Brady is coming around a little more. He's being respectful to me and his father ever since the brothers were attacked. I don't know if it just scared him, knowing how far Byron is willing to go, or what. But he's coming around.

"You know he's not trying to impress anyone who's not Charleigh, Mom." Brady loves to tease Johnny about the one woman my sweet boy will never have. It's not because he isn't handsome or a good man, but because he has crushed on this particular woman since he first laid eyes on her at the tender age of ten. She's his therapist's daughter, not to mention almost eleven years older than him.

"Now, Brady—what did I tell you about teasing your brother about his little crush?"

Johnny huffs, throwing his hands into the air. "There you go, too, Mama. Damn. I'm a grown-ass man now. I don't do crushes. I'll have what I want, wait and see, both of you." He stomps off, sulking, causing us to laugh.

"Awe, big brother, don't cry," Brady yells. He gets a "fuck you" in return.

"Hey! Watch your mouth, young man. You ain't too big to get your ass whooped," I yell down the hallway before falling again into laughter with my baby boy.

We are all in the main room where the bar is. I don't think I'll ever get used to my boys seeing all of these half-naked women dancing and doing sexual favors for the brothers right in front of everyone. It's unquestionably awkward.

Brady goes over to play pool with Memphis and Navy,

so I go to the jukebox to pick out a few songs. It has a few of my favorites—usually not what one would put in a jukebox. I'm thinking that maybe someone had them put on with me in mind.

I sway my hips as the melody of The Animals' 'House of The Rising Sun' begins to play. It's an amazing song and certainly one of my favorites. I walk to the bar and grab myself a drink when Navy approaches and gets a drink for herself.

"Brady is a really good kid, they both are good boys. You did good, Mama." She nudges me with her hip, making me smile.

"Thank you. I like to think so."

We sit and drink together for about forty-five minutes, or however long it took us to get shit-faced because that is exactly what we are right now.

"Sis, how much have you had to drink?" Capone asks Navy.

This results in a bout of giggles, pissing Capone off. "Dammit, Memphis, get over here and get your woman. She's three sheets, man."

We laugh as Memphis shakes his head. "No way, bro. You remember what happened the last time I tried to take her alcohol away. If she gets sick, she might finally learn her damn limit."

Capone doesn't like his response but doesn't press the issue.

Navy's face sobers a bit as she slides closer to me. "Look, Layla, these kut sluts have to learn their place. Sometimes it's our job to put them there, so don't hesitate to protect what's yours."

I must be really drunk because I'm not understanding and, evidently, it shows. Navy throws her chin up in the direction behind us. I turn around not knowing what to expect.

Straight away I see red.

A tall, skinny woman is standing in front of Tank, rubbing up and down his thighs while he sits talking to Tats and Snoopy. Only her ass is covered with a thin pair of panties—her upper half is bare and shoved in his face.

"Fuck, Memphis, I told you this shit was gonna happen. Your ol' lady is over here stirring the shit pot. Now shit is gonna hit the fan." Capone's overly-dramatic reaction causes Memphis to laugh.

"Damn, Pone, what did you do? Pick up a how-to-speak-like-a-Southerner-for-dummies handbook? I mean, really. Stirring the shit pot? Who says that shit?"

Everyone is laughing, but the anger I feel won't let me join in. My feet are moving before I realize what I'm doing.

"Fucking, fuck. Navy, you need to do something."

I hear her tell Capone he's right, before yelling at the bartender, "I need two more shots, babe. Oh, and if you've got any popcorn, that'd be great. I always love popcorn while watching a good show."

Her comment makes me smile slightly, so I'm sure I look a wee bit crazy as I approach Tank.

Tats and Snoop look up to see me coming. They both scatter, causing Tank to turn his beautiful face in my direction.

I stand in front of a very intoxicated Tank. His eyes

are glossy and glazed over as he smirks at me. Red doesn't notice me at first until she twists around to grind on his lap. Her head pops up as she makes a comment about him taking her to his room. Her eyes go wide as she realizes I'm standing there. She stops dancing and stands up, stepping close to me. I look past her to Tank and watch as he puts both arms up on the back of the couch. He then cocks his head to the side, wearing the same smirk, as if he's trying to get a rise out of me.

He wants to see what I do, how I handle the situation.

"Do you mind, shorty? I'm trying to get off tonight, so why don't you just skedaddle." She makes a hand motion, telling me to go away.

I grab her hand and twist it behind her back. Her wrist snaps as I jerk it up further. She screams and calls me a bitch, and a few other names, as I walk her half-naked ass to the door. I throw her out. "You won't be getting laid by Tank ever again as long as I exist, bitch. You need to keep that needy snatch of yours out here until it cools down. It's Corset, right?"

She makes to speak, but me being the bitch I am, I interrupt her, "It doesn't matter, you will always be a bitch to me—words from the wise, bitch. Stay the fuck away from Tank or I will fucking end you. This is me being nice, don't push me." I slam the door shut and lock it. She'll be fine, it's not like we'll get any snow tonight. It is Georgia, after all.

Navy is on me as soon as I turn around. "That's why we are gonna be best friends. We are some bad bitches for sure. That's how I'd handle shit, too. So classy."

Capone and Memphis are looking at her as if she has

lost her mind.

"You do remember what you've done in your lifetime, right? Nothing was classy about that shit, sis." Capone says with a smirk.

She looks at them like she's going through it in her head. "Well, exactly how classy can you be while dismembering a body, asshole?"

I laugh out loud, causing everyone to look at me. "Wait—you dismembered someone, like, for real?" I wait, but no one speaks. "Dammit, Navy, why are you holding out on me? I need you to teach me, so I can dismember some of my baby's daddy's parts if he ever sticks them anywhere near that skanky-ass whore again." I turn to see him right behind me.

He stops, his glass midway to his mouth. Grimacing, he grabs his crotch. I smile, knowing my words were understood.

"Mom, what the hell? You do know I'm still here, right? That is shit a child should never have to hear about his parents. Damn, that's nasty." With that, he walks off, as does everyone else, letting us have a moment.

"Is this what goes on here every night? You, fucking different women every chance you get?"

He looks at me with so much fire, so much sexiness it makes my thighs clench. Of course, he notices, smiling. "I knew you were watching me, shortcake. I needed to see how much you wanted me, or if you even wanted me at all."

He comes closer, so close I can smell the whiskey on his breath. "Did you get the answers you were looking for? The answers you wanted?" I ask.

He closes the distance and kisses me slowly before dropping his glass on the floor so he can wrap both arms around my thighs. Picking me up as if I weigh nothing at all, he squeezes my ass as he walks us down the hall to his room. After the door slams, my back is against it.

"From the time your favorite song hit those speakers to the first sway of your hips as you started to dance you had my eyes, all of my attention, shortcake."

"All these years have passed, yet looking at you like this right now, it's as if no time at all has gone by. You're still as beautiful as you were that very first night I saw you. Your little black dress with those sexy red heels. These dark, racy curls flowing down your back. You had my attention already, but when you looked up at me with those big, beautiful eyes and full, pink lips, I was a goner."

My eyes water at the fact that after all of these years he still remembers me the way I remember him. I pull his face close, pressing my lips to his. "I've missed you so much, baby."

No more words are spoken as he takes me to the bed, stripping me of every article of clothing, before disrobing himself. He starts at my feet, kissing his way up my body slowly, waking up feelings I didn't think were possible for me anymore.

"Layla, baby, I need you to be a very good girl for me tonight. Don't move or I'll go even slower, postponing that orgasm I know you're so eager for. I haven't had the pleasure of smelling, tasting, or loving this beautiful body in way too long, and tonight, I'm gonna do just that."

TANK

I lick slowly up and down her sweet slit, not parting her lips. Her body is responding perfectly—writhing and making those little whimpers that drive me insane, letting me know she needs this just as much, if not more than I do.

"Why, baby? Why did you have to push me away?" I mumble between licks as I look up at her.

Her eyes water with sadness, yet her face is flushed with need, making her even more beautiful. "I loved you, shortcake, so much."

She doesn't respond, so I lick my way up her belly until I'm met with her still-perky tits. Her plump, dusty-rose nipples wait patiently for my lips. I don't disappoint as I place my lips around each one, giving them a nice tug with my teeth. She screams out in pleasure.

"Zane, baby, please. Please."

I suck and bite up her collarbone to her ear as I take the

head of my cock and rub it against her wet cunt. Mixing both of our juices, I pop the tip in and remove it just as quickly, making her eyes light with fire.

"What's the matter, baby? Do I have something you need?" I smirk, not expecting her to return with a smirk of her own, but she does, which catches me by surprise. I don't see it coming when she grabs my cock and raises up, pushing me onto my back.

"Yes, you have something I need."

Now on my back with my very hard dick sticking straight up, only becoming harder with every pulse, she twirls her tongue around it, lapping up every bit of pre-come before licking up and down the veiny under part of my shaft. "Fuck, baby, you always did know how to suck me off. Yes, I fucking missed this. Your puffy wet lips wrapped tightly around me. Ah, yeah, listen to you gag, shortcake. So fucking perfect."

She turns around and sits her soaked pussy down on my face while continuing to suck and lick my cock and balls without missing a beat. I don't hesitate, shoving my face into her beautiful cunt, fucking her tight holes with my tongue.

"Zane, Zane, baby."

I'm not sure when she stopped sucking me, but she's now gripping my headboard, bouncing like a motherfucking porn star on my tongue.

I know the moment she's about to come—from screaming my name, the shaking of her thighs, to the gush that soaks my mouth. "You better hold the fuck on, Layla, because I'm about to own this fucking pussy."

I get up and out of the bed and slam her back against the wall. As bad as I wanted to go slow with her tonight, she ruined that shit the minute she started choking on my cock. "Dammit, Layla, you couldn't just let me take it slow, could you?"

I slam my cock inside her hard and rough, causing her to throw her head back and hit the wall. It doesn't phase her at all. She's fucking up my back and my ass as she scratches her nails into my skin. She wants me deeper into her needy body.

"Tell me, Layla, has anyone fucked you the way I do? Huh? Tell me." I pull her off my cock and spin her around. "Hands on the fucking wall." I grab a handful of hair and slap her perfectly round ass before ramming in deep.

"Ah, oh my God, Zane. I need it, I need you baby. No, no one has ever made my pussy feel the way you do. Please."

I love when she begs. "Whose pussy is this, shortcake? Who the fuck do you belong to—have always fucking belonged to?" I feel myself about to explode, so I reach down and rub her swollen clit as I continue to plunge deep. "Touch your toes, now!"

She goes down, which lets my cock go even deeper. She screams my name over and over again while coming. I yank her hair still wrapped around my hand as I cover the walls of her pussy with my seed.

* * *

Watching her sleep brings back so many good memories, and with her warm body snuggled so close to mine, I'm sure I will get some much-needed rest tonight. "Goodnight, shortcake." I kiss her sweet lips before passing out.

TANK

Age Eighteen

"**W**hat's up, B? I told you I had a lot of shit to do and would call you as soon as I could."

He's silent for a few minutes, and I'm starting to think I've hurt his feelings again, which makes me feel like shit, but it's the only way to protect him. If it wasn't for his ragged breathing I would think he'd hung up on me—wouldn't be the first time.

"Brady, you still there, man? You okay?"

I'm about to get upset and then he speaks, changing my whole fucking path in life, "I don't feel anything, Zane. No pain or anything. So, where is all the blood coming from?"

TANK

"**N**o. No! Brady, please wake up. Wake up, man. I'm sorry, I'm so fucking sorry. Please wake up."

I hear my shortcake in the distance, yelling for me. Following the sound of her voice, my eyes pop open.

She's sitting on me, holding my face. "Zane, baby, are you okay? You were screaming in your sleep about Brady."

I gently raise her off me and grab my phone off the nightstand. I never have these dreams unless he's been heavy on my mind or it's getting close to his birthday. I look at the time and date—his birthday is next fucking week. When will this shit stop? When will the guilt fade? "Fuck." I drop my head, running my fingers through my hair, and I feel her slide up behind me.

"It's not your fault, Zane. He would have never wanted this for you—this guilt you allow to eat you alive."

"How the fuck would you know, Layla? You never knew him. You don't know what our relationship was like. He was just a kid who needed his brother and I let him the fuck down. Maybe our son was lucky not to have me in his life, fuck. If I couldn't even keep my thirteen-year-old brother alive, how the fuck would I have kept my child alive all these years?"

I'm up and on my way to wash the sweat from my face and neck when Layla's voice stops me in my tracks.

She practically yells, "Don't you dare fucking say that, you dumbass. You were a fucking child yourself, trying to provide for your baby brother and yourself the best you knew how. So you don't get to belittle who you were in his life. You. Were. His. Protector. Just like you would have been in our son's life.

"I wanted you there, in his life, our life. He would at least know what a loving family felt like. Hell, I fucked up any vision he may have had of a happy family with my shitty choice in men. He would have loved you—us together as a family.

"We are human, mistakes will always be made, Zane, but we are not bad fucking people, so stop trying to convince yourself otherwise."

* * *

The thudding on the door brings me out of my sleep and on high alert. I grab my .38 special out of the nightstand. As I throw the covers back and jump up, readying myself for anything, I hear the sweetest little voice as the tapping noise starts again.

"Unk Tank, Unk Tank," My beautiful little niece calls, slapping on my door.

I rush to open the door. She's standing there, her wild curls all over her head, smiling.

"Up." She reaches her chubby little hands up above her head.

"Hey, my little princess, what are you doing out here by yourself?"

She shrugs her little shoulders. "Unk Pone."

I love the way she says our names. "You can't find Uncle Capone, sweet girl, is that what it is? Come on, I'll help you find him." It's barely light outside, but I know Navy is awake and probably making breakfast, she always does when they stay the night at the clubhouse, which is often.

"Capone, oh, Capone. Where are you?" I say in a sing-song tone.

He comes around the corner fast, like someone is chasing his ass. "There you are, princess. I've been looking everywhere for you. Don't scare Unk Pone like that again, okay, pretty?" He grabs her from my arms, kissing her chubby cheeks. "Thanks, man, I set her down for just a few seconds to make a cup of coffee then turned around and she was gone."

I tell him it's not a big deal, I always love seeing her beautiful face. Well, when it's not covered by all the curls, that is. I let him know I need him to inform the rest of the officers I'll need them in church around nine fifteen to talk about the last few shipments of guns that need to go out as soon as possible. A few runs will be coming up, and we're gonna need extra protection until we find this Byron asshole and any puppets he's got coming our way.

LAYLA

L ast week I thought we had a breakthrough, but Tank is being grumpier than before, and it can't be from the lack of sex. I can't seem to get enough of him, his body on top of mine is my favorite pass time. I can't figure out what's going on with him though, and it's starting to affect my mood as well. I know last week they had to go on some runs and he was worried about his men being safe, as well as us being safe here.

Today is the last run for a while if the conversation I was eavesdropping on is factual. I wasn't aware they owned any clubs or auto repair garages until this morning. Apparently, Blissful Climax is their newest addition—a strip club. I don't know how I feel about that, but I guess we will find out because this weekend we're supposed to go to tryouts. *We* because when I learned of Tank's plans I knew there was absolutely no way he was going to watch some naked women audition. No way, *period*. So I volunteered my services, and of course, he laughed before saying, "Sure, babe."

"Mom, what's on the agenda while the brothers are on this run?" Johnny says as he and Brady sit down beside me on the couch.

"I'm not sure, but I would like to know where the hell my two boys have been hiding. I feel like I never see you anymore." I give them my sincerest frowny face.

"Well, I just been out and about with the brothers. Brady over here has been working in the shop with Tats, learning to fix cars and shit. Ain't that right, little bro." Johnny nudges him.

"Yeah, Mom, I really like it here with the guys, and I'm learning a lot from them, especially Tats."

As if he senses he's being talked about, Tats walks into the room, smoking a blunt, along with Tank and Capone.

"Damn that smells good; let me get a hit."

Johnny asking for the weed totally catches me of guard. My eyes are as wide as saucers, I'm sure.

"What's wrong, Mom? Weed is natural. It's an herb, from the earth."

I nod, knowing he's right and, if I'm being honest, I always loved a good smoke session myself. I guess seeing your kids do it hits you a little differently though.

"Can I get a hit?"

All heads turn to my youngest son.

As I'm saying no, his father tells him yes.

"Excuse me, but I think he's too damn young to smoke weed, Zane."

He finishes his turn then passes it to Tats. "I agree a hundred percent, shortcake, however, he is at the age now to know if he wants to try something, and nine times out of ten they will do it with or without our permission. I would rather him do it, or anything that he has his mind set on trying, right here in front of me, so I can protect and help him if the reaction is more than he can handle or not what he expects."

I think we're all just wondering where the fuck that came from.

"Damn, Tats, what the hell you got me smoking on? I'm sounding all dad-like and shit, giving out parental advice."

We all laugh, but looking into Zane's eyes, I understand he needs this with his son. So, I nod and take a hit from the blunt before passing it to Brady. I leave the boys to do their thing while I go find some snacks for later.

TANK

"**A**ll right, boys, are we ready for this last drop? Let's make it quick and painless, paying close attention to our surroundings at all times. This buyer is an asshole and Frank, our usual buyer, didn't want to deal with him personally. So, I told him that as long as he knew the buyer and the guy was a straight shooter like Frank himself the Guardians would drop off the shipment for him. And of course, he paid us a little extra to do so. This is the last of the guns, so we can try our luck at running on the straight and narrow.

"Capone, Snoop, Memphis, and Tats we'll be riding, Crow will be transporting the guns in the cage. Scar and the other prospects will stay here with the women and kids along with the rest of the members. Make sure to wear your vests under your clothes because these motherfuckers could pop up at any time. Be focused and motherfucking ready."

I kiss Layla, letting her know I'm sorry for being so grumpy and out of it this past week. I tell the boys that when I get back we'll start talking more about what they want in life, so if possible, I can make that happen for them. I hope they choose to stay after all is said and done.

"Oh, before I forget, here's a burner so I can reach you and vice versa. Don't make any calls unless it's to me or a brother, understand?" I slap her ass, making her yelp before I throw on my Teflon vest, thermal, then my kut. My colors are always showing, no matter where I go.

* * *

We finally get to our destination, not far from the country-ass town where Layla was living. It's an old, worn-down, and rusted warehouse.

"You sure this is the right spot, Tank?" Capone asks as the clanking of chains slam against the old garage-type door.

It starts to rise. Standing behind it is a big-ass bald dude with a mean mug and an AK-47.

"Why the fuck is he rocking an AK for a drop this small?" I look over at Crow in the van beside us as he takes the words right out of my mouth.

"You must be Eagle." I walk toward him, making sure to keep my eyes on his trigger finger.

"I guess that makes you Tank. Now that we're fucking acquainted why don't you show me the shit."

I tilt my head, wondering if he knows who the fuck he's talking to. He mirrors my expression, and I know in my gut he's gonna be a problem for me. I motion for Crow to back the van under the raised door. I hit the side when he goes further than my liking.

"Let's just make this quick as it seems you're not too happy to see us. Show me our money and the boys will gladly unload the boxes."

All of my men walk up behind me, and Eagle laughs. I don't recall saying anything funny, so what the fuck is this guy's deal? One thing's for certain, Frank was not lying about this guy being an asshole.

I hear the rattle of chains and something that sounds like a muffled scream.

"Shut that bitch up, Blaze," Eagle yells upward never taking his eyes off of us. I hear the sound again, followed by the familiar sound of biker boots.

I follow the sound and see a girl in a fucking cage hanging on the second floor. Her face is red and swollen and she has a gag in her mouth which explains why her screaming was so muffled. "I don't think I like what you're into, man."

He raises his gun, causing a chain reaction. We all stand, with our guns pointed at each other as about ten other men come out of the woodwork and stand at his back. "No one fucking asked you, fuck face." With his firepower, he could easily take us out. But he doesn't have the brains to understand his time is now over.

I'm not a stupid man and always like to have a backup plan, which is why Capone came in through the back, placing some pretty potent explosives throughout this shithole. He now stands behind these men with nice little balls that go *boom* in his hands.

Eagle could pull that trigger taking us all out, but he and his men won't be far behind when my little pyromaniac lights those fuses.

"You see, I am a man who always expects the worst and hopes for the best. Something about your demeanor set me off from the beginning. I knew you were gonna piss me off. Now, tell your boy to unlock the cage and take the fucking handcuffs off of her, the gag too, motherfucker. Or I'm blowing this bitch to kingdom come. Your choice."

That sly-ass smile is no longer in place, but replacing it is a look of confusion.

"I don't understand the confusion here, Eagle. I mean, it's pretty much a you-do-this-shit-or-I'm-gonna-do-that-shit-boom-motherfucker kind of thing."

I watch with a smile as he yells for Blaze to let her go, but when he looks back at me, I can see it—a hint of a smile.

"You're making a huge mistake, asshole, and you don't even know it. But you will soon enough."

All of his men have now been disarmed by Tats and Capone. Tats has the girl wrapped tightly under his arm, walking back to me, while Capone goes back in the direction from which he came.

"Tank, I remember those kuts from Podunk, that country hell I was in, looking for Jamison."

We walk backward to our rides, making sure no one makes any sudden moves when his words register. I don't know what my tell was, but Eagle saw something and begins to laugh, a husky, two-packs-a-day kinda laugh.

"You catching on now, motherfucker." Eagles says.

As soon as we are far enough away, and Capone is back around front and on his bike, he looks over to the bastard laughing and winks before saying, "Boom."

His eyes go wide as he yells for them to run, but it's too late. One explosion after another goes off, sending debris flying everywhere, and just as I'm about to call Layla, a torso lands directly on the windshield of the van Crow's in right beside us.

"Damn, that's nasty as hell, Capone," Crow says, putting window cleaner on the windshield and turning on the wipers. As if that will take care of the mess.

Capone is unable to control his laughter because it's smearing the blood and burnt pieces of flesh everywhere. "I swear, man, you're so damn childish. Get this shit off my ride. Fuck."

My phone rings and the caller ID pops up as "unknown." It has to be Layla.

"Hey, shortcake, we're on our way back." I hear a slight whimper before a growl.

"Well, well, Tank. It looks like Shortcake, here, will be coming to stay with me for a while, so I can use her up until I tire of her frigid-ass and decide to kill her. Tell him, Layla. You've made a choice and that choice is me."

I hear my girl's whimper before she comes onto the phone. "It's okay, Zane. Just promise me you'll take care of our boys and make sure they have all they need. I'll be fine, just let me go."

I'm furious at her words, though I know they are completely forced, I hate hearing them come from her beautiful mouth. It reminds me of long ago when similar words were used to push me away. "No, Layla, not this time. You can't push me away a second time. I won't let you."

I hear her scream before being disconnected.

"Motherfucker!" I roar before hauling ass back to see how the fuck this man got into my domain and took what belongs to me.

LAYLA

"**I** should kill you right now, you stupid little cunt, for all of the trouble I've had to go through to find you. Did you really think you could get away from me, Layla? Haven't you learned yet? No one gets away from me unless they're wearing a toe tag, and that's only if they get lucky. Most of them don't even make it to the morgue. I make sure all ways of identifying the body are removed before taking apart the rest and spreading it across different counties." His laugh is sickening.

My stomach twists. The contents from the day are not far from coming up.

"Why won't you just let me go? What do I have that makes you want to keep me around? I have nothing, Byron! For fuck's sake—I'm a broke mother of two, why you won't let me go?" I look him right in his evil, dark eyes and see nothing there—no love, no remorse or sadness, just complete emptiness.

"Oh, Layla, you have something of worth to me, but it has nothing to do with you personally. You just have shit luck and bad taste in men."

That comment only confuses me further as to why the fuck I'm here. "Tell me, then, why did you beat me and my kids all those years, and after every attempt at leaving, you used my children against me to make sure I stayed? Why? It makes no sense."

He looks at me for a moment as if contemplating what he wants to say. "Well, I guess being as you're going to die either way, it won't hurt if I tell you the truth. You possess Tank's heart and always have, so hurting you hurts him. Keeping you away from him all these years hurt him. Making sure he didn't know he had a son hurt him, which brings me pure pleasure. And when I kill you, it will bring him to his knees as he did me all those years ago."

What in the actual fuck is going on here? He's talking in fucking circles and I'm more lost now than before. "So, you knew Tank when he was younger and he took something from you that was important. Is that what you're saying? Because if it is that still doesn't explain beating me and my innocent kids."

This makes him angry. He slings a metal bar at me, hitting me across both legs tied to the bottom of the chair. I scream out at the intensity of the pain, then puke off to the side. It still gets on my clothes because my hands are tied, preventing me from moving anything but my head.

"Jeremy was fucking innocent, too!" he yells while pacing the room, throwing things around.

I have no idea where we are, but I know it's not far from the Guardians' clubhouse. The room is huge. It almost looks like an old barn or garage. "Who is Jeremy?"

The question makes him stop pacing and squat down in front of me. He squeezes my face so hard I can taste blood, which threatens the remaining contents of my stomach. "Jeremy was my fucking brother and my only friend. That piece of shit, Tank, killed my little brother with God knows what type of knife, mutilating his body beyond recognition before dumping him in the trashcan outside of my parents' place like he was nothing. He took away my life that day, and I've been working every day since to make sure I take away his."

"I've already got his little sister caged up in my warehouse. She'll die a brutal death before I shove her in a trashcan outside the entrance gate of his compound. Then I'll hit him where it hurts when I take your bloody body and discard you like a piece of trash on his doorstep. When he opens the door, I'll be there watching, enjoying him experience the pain of losing someone he loves, before I take his now-worthless life."

A fucking psychopath—that is all I can come up with to describe this guy after that shit story. I didn't even know Tank had a sister. "I don't understand, how do you know he was the one who killed your brother? And if you're so sure, why wasn't he incarcerated?"

His laugh is sardonic as he jumps up and begins to pace once again. "You see, that's the reason I became an officer. There are too many cops who don't investigate properly. Every time they questioned Tank, his alibi was the same.

His sergeant at arms said they were both in Memphis Tennessee visiting a friend of his. There was no way to prove otherwise. The friend supposedly confirmed it true and no murder weapon was ever found, so they ended the investigation on him just like that.

"I know he's guilty. Jeremy told me when his friends started mysteriously disappearing one by one that if anything happened to him it would be at the hands of Tank."

"You can't actually believe you could just take the word of an out-of-control teen who probably had plenty of enemies."

He screams out. The back of his hand connects with my face, making me see spots. Before I can get my vision back, the other hand slams across my face and head. Emptying what's left in my stomach is the last thing I remember before the darkness takes me.

TANK

"**S**o, you're saying he and his boys just waltzed into my fucking clubhouse with a search warrant?" I cannot believe this shit. "On what fucking grounds? This isn't his fucking jurisdiction. He has no damn right to invade our home, none at all. Truth be told, it was probably a fake-ass warrant, and he should have been shot on fucking sight."

Scar steps up, followed by Johnny, and a visually upset Brady, who catches me off guard by hugging me. "How are we gonna get my mama back, Zane? I can't lose her, she's all I've got. Fuck! I've been nothing but a little shit to her lately, and if anything happens to her I'll never forgive myself." He holds his tears back to look strong in front of us, but I know the kid is fucking heartbroken.

"Look at me. You have me, your brother, and all of my brothers. We will get your mom back and Jamison will never be a threat to her or my boys again."

He looks skeptical at first, but the more I assure him she will be coming home and everything will be fine he comes around. Now, if I can only convince myself I can get to her in time.

"No one could shoot them, Tank, they had red dots coming from so many different directions. I never knew there could be so much corruption in one place, but he showed me different tonight." I think that's the most I've heard Scar speak since Dodger died.

"Byron is a calculating psychopath, he's ruthless and non-caring unless it pertains to him or works out in his favor. He will take down anything and anyone who gets in the way of his objective," her voice is weak and strained, but I hear her words perfectly. The girl we rescued from the warehouse sits on the couch with her head down as she speaks, "Our father was murdered, so Byron knew my protection was limited. He took me from my twentieth birthday party."

So, they're related. What the fuck is up with this family? "You're related to the asshole who took my ol' lady?"

Immediately, her head shakes. "No." She looks up at me for the first time and I have to catch my fucking breath. With green eyes that match mine, she stares at me. "I'm related to you, Zane. I'm your half-sister, Melanie."

I must be fucking hearing things. "Excuse me? My what?" I don't have time for bullshit right now, I've got to find my woman.

"Asmodeus was our father, the President of the Demons and a son of a bitch, but at least I was protected by the club when he was alive. No one would have done the things to me that have been done. I've been beaten and sexually abused for weeks until he was ready to carry out his plans. At first, I thought I was to be sold like some of the other girls, but I found out that his plans for me were a little different. I was to die by his hands, and after being beat to death, he was going to throw me into your trashcan at the gate entrance of your clubhouse. I overheard him say you would understand his message loud and clear. Do you know what he's talking about, Zane?"

I stumble backward as if someone punched me in the face. I can't breathe. How can she know the details of that night? How does he know? Who the fuck is this man?

"Tank, brother, are you okay? What does all of that shit mean? What message would you have understood by that sick shit he was planning?" Snoopy is in my face, making it harder to breathe.

I push him back, bolt to my room, and lock the door. I go to my closet and drop down to my knees in front of the black box that holds the very weapon my brother took his life with—the same weapon I used to kill the pieces of shit responsible for his death.

TANK

The Past

"**W**hat are you talking about, Brady? What blood?"

I hear Jeremy and the boys laugh beside me, then say Brady must be tripping hard on the drugs he gave him earlier.

"What the fuck!" I scream as I take off running. "Brady, buddy, are you there? Stay on the phone, okay. I'm not far." I hear things breaking and his breathing becomes more rapid.

"I can't get it out, Zane. It's like it's crawling inside of me. I want it out of my body, but nothing comes out except more blood."

Oh my God, no, please no. "Brady, can you just sit down for me and breathe? I'm almost home. Please, man, put down whatever you have in your hands, okay? Don't hurt yourself, please, bro." I hear a loud thud then nothing but silence.

"Brady! Brady! Bro, please pick up the phone! Please!" I call 911 and run faster than I've ever run. Where is that bitch of a mother? How can she not hear the constant breaking and clattering? Please be okay, Brady.

I bust through the front door and, just as I thought, my mother is passed out on the couch, unable to hear a damn thing.

"Brady!"

His door is cracked and I see blood on the knob. I push it open. Nothing could have prepared me for the scene inside. Blood on the walls, the bed, and all over the TV screen and controller where he was obviously playing a game.

"Brady, where are you, buddy?" I hear a gurgle from the bathroom and know then that my life will forever be changed.

Brady's body lays on the floor in pools of blood. I lift his head onto my lap and beg him to open his eyes. "Please, Brady, wake up. Wake up, bro. I love you, B. Please, I love you. Don't go." I cry more than any boy or man should until the paramedics and officers pull him out of my arms. That's when the anger sets in and I start planning my revenge.

My mother, if you can call her that, went to jail for child neglect but spent no time at all as long as she enrolled in classes to help with her addiction. After she went through the whole drug program, her probation dropped. She ended up relapsing. She started getting pills from my Uncle Benny, which then turned into meth. Large amounts of money added up and she couldn't pay it back. No one gets away with not paying Benny, so he killed my mother. In return, I killed him and the majority of his club, taking over this city as president of my own MC.

The Guardian Angels were born.

LAYLA

Freezing water hits my face and body, making me scream and jolt. My chair tilts over. I'm unable to catch myself because I'm still tied down and my head hits the floor hard, making my eyes close again. Agony, pure fucking agony, is what I'm feeling right now.

"Wake up, bitch. It's time to make a call. I can't wait to see how bent out of shape our boy Tank is knowing you're with me. Things were supposed to go a little differently, but since he blew up my warehouse and saved his pathetic sister, I guess we'll be moving on to plan B. We're going to taunt him a bit, you know, have a little fun before I cut you up and send him the pieces.

"Oh, I know what will be fun, but first you need to clean up. You stink." He pulls me by my hair, letting my chair scrape across the floor as he drags me to something similar to a shower.

He puts me under the spray of the water to get the dried vomit off of me as well as the urine because he refuses to untie me to go to the restroom. The water shuts off and he tells me it's time to make a phone call that will make things a little more interesting. "Then you'll sit there and dry until it's time to play."

TANK

"**P**rez, open this fucking door or we're breaking this shit down. I'll get Pone to get one of his grenades. Don't fucking try me." Snoop is a ballsy bastard for speaking to me like that, but I understand his urgency.

I close the closet and as I'm opening the door I'm met with a hallway full of concerned brothers. My phone rings. "Hello, Layla? Layla, is that you?"

Byron laughs on the other end of the line. "Awe, you sound so concerned, Tank. Are you, concerned?" More laughing.

I squeeze the phone hard enough for it to crack. Capone jerks it out of my hand and puts it on speaker. "What is it that you want, Jamison?"

He hums as if he's thinking about how he wants to answer. "Well, I want revenge, of course. I want you to pay for what you did, so I've decided to cut off one piece of this beautiful body at a time and have it delivered to you piece by beautiful piece until you admit it and produce the weapon it was done with. I'll start taking off pieces tomorrow night at, oh, say, eight o'clock. That's a good time for you, right?"

It's the time my brother took his last breath, so I made sure that was their time of death too. "Which one?" I ask him.

"Excuse me?" he tries to act dumb.

"Which one was it? Which one was worth you hurting my family for all of these years?"

A growl leaves his body before he yells through the phone. "My fucking brother, Jeremy. You killed the only person in my life who meant something to me, you son of a bitch."

I do remember a brief conversation about a brother in college but never saw him. "He killed mine, too, motherfucker."

* * *

Curious and expecting eyes stare at me in the small confines of this hallway, making me feel like I'm suffocating. I do not like closed-in spaces, they make me panic, which is happening now. My heart rate picks up and my hands begin to shake. It's a feeling I'm all too familiar with. "Look, as soon as we get out of this hallway we can talk, but not before then." I push through as I spout off things that need to be done, "Crow, get Dane on the phone. I need to know anything and everything about that last call—if it pinged on any of the cell towers in our vicinity, anywhere close by. I need to know if any property has been recently bought or rented. ASAP."

He's already dialing before I finish.

"Capone, get in touch with Officer Mike. I need to know if he knows of any locations near us that Jamison could be using to keep Layla in." I have to get myself under control so I can think clearly. Visions of that night keep invading my mind.

TANK

The Past

"**D**on't fucking kill me, Zane! How in the fuck was I supposed to know he would trip that fucking hard? It was just a small dose of phencyclidine, man. He shouldn't have fucking killed himself." Jeremy's screams fill the air as the sharp blade slices through his stomach.

"You knew he was a thirteen-year-old kid and my fucking brother!"

He throws his hands up. "Please, please don't kill—" he doesn't finish as the blade slices through again, making defensive wounds on the hands he tries to block with. Blood pours from his mouth.

Seven fifty-eight. I slice more until my watch alarms me that it's eight PM. I hear his gurgle of death as the last slice splits his throat open.

LAYLA

"**B**yron, I need food and to use the restroom, please. I'm not feeling so well."

He sneers in my direction. "Well, let's hope you don't go and die before I get the opportunity to fucking kill you." He turns back around, doing something on his phone.

The sickness I'm feeling is somewhat familiar. I felt something like this when I was pregnant with Brady, but not this early. I think I was around three months. It was right after Tank left that I found out I was pregnant, that it wasn't just a virus as I expected. It's only been about six or seven weeks since my first time with Zane again. God, what if I'm pregnant? Please help keep our baby safe until I get out of here.

"Dammit, Byron, it took us forever to get back down here, man. Lieutenant had us moving the girls to another location. He seems to think since Melanie got away, she's gonna talk."

How many crooked-ass cops can fit into this damn barn? I know those voices and hate them both. They'd both put their filthy hands on me while I was restrained, with Byron sitting in the corner watching. His need for control and power has ruined him. That and the fact he's just fucking crazy.

I try to listen without them noticing, in case they give anything as to where those poor girls may be. God only knows what they've had to endure while in the hands of these monsters.

"Where the hell did you take them? You know I have multiple buyers coming in two days. Shit! I hate when he makes decisions without consulting me first," Byron says angrily.

He's beyond angry, pacing back and forth, tapping his finger on his chin. "As soon as I get rid of this bitch and Tank, my brother's soul can rest and we can get back to making this money. I may have to move up the time on executing my plan so we can get back into town before the buyers show."

"I think your right, Jamison. I don't care for the girls' new location. It's not as private as we would like. Honestly, I think it's a bit risky, but who am I to argue with the Lieutenant. They're all tied up in the basement of his wife's restaurant, and even though it's pretty much secluded and away from other businesses, I still think it's a bit precarious."

I recognize this voice as Donavan. He is always more aggressive than the others made to watch my every move.

I'm sure Byron got off on watching him abuse me.

"So, do we at least get to have a little hard-core play session with the bitch before we cut her up?"

Laughter fills the room.

"Oh, I think that sounds like a great idea, boys. I am wound pretty tight. A nice hard release sounds good."

Please find me, Zane, please.

TANK

I'm waiting patiently for someone to come through with some intel I can fucking use. I have to find Layla and fast before this damn psycho starts taking her apart. Dane and Mike are both on their way over, hopefully with something useful or I might just lose my shit. Between this shit and my brother's birthday tomorrow, I'm in a fucked up headspace. Not to mention, I have a sister who knew my piece of shit father.

"Melanie, right? How is it that you know about me, yet I've never met my sperm donor and never knew I had a sister? You said you just turned twenty, so how old was our old man?"

She looks at me. Tats is at her side, acting as if I'm unpredictable or some shit. I would never hurt my damn sister.

"He was sixty-five when he was murdered a few months ago. Did your mom ever tell you about him, or their relationship?"

I shake my head. That was a subject she never touched. She always said I was a blessing from God and that's all that mattered. She did talk a little about Brady's father though, as we had different dads.

"Are you sure you want to hear about it? Because from the description I overheard one night while they were all drunk, it's not one I would want to hear about my mother."

I look at her and it's crazy how much her eyes are like mine. "Go ahead, nothing you could say can be any worse than the shit I've lived or seen."

She takes a deep breath before she begins, "Well, the night I found out about you I was at a patch party, so of course, everyone was drunk and talking shit. I was never allowed in the main room when parties were going on, but this particular night I knew everyone was shit-faced, so I went down to fix something to drink.

"On my way to the kitchen, I heard Mammon, the club vice president, ask dad about his boy. Curious, because I could have a brother, I listened in. Asmodeus told him you were now the president of the Guardian Angels and that your road name was Tank. They laughed about how different your clubs were—they were demons and you were angels. He then went on to talk about how you came about and that your mother never told him. I thought that was so messed up until Mammon's next words.

"He told him he wouldn't tell either if he was—" she stops then looks around the room at all of the eyes on her, visibly becoming nervous.

I touch her hand. "It's okay, you are and always will be

safe here."

She nods and leaves her head down as she finishes, "He told him he wouldn't tell either if he'd gotten pregnant after being brutally raped by the president of the Demons. They laughed as they went into detail about the things done to your mother. He said he saw her around town a few months later and realized he'd possibly left a Demon seed in her. So, he followed her, kept eyes on her until after you were born. He wanted to see your features, see if you carried any of his. He knew immediately you were his because you had his eyes, our eyes. He said he watched you from a distance until one day she saw him.

"He approached her and asked to see you. He could see she had been self-medicating. She started screaming at him about him raping her and ruining her life. Told him the least he could do was support her fucking habit since it was his fault she had to stay high on pills to get through her day."

A hundred different emotions run through me, but I see in her eyes that she's not finished just yet.

"He also mentioned you had an uncle named Benny, who was a Demon as well but from another chapter. He and our father were supplying your mother with her drug of choice until she got pregnant with Brady. Then she stopped for a while, but it didn't last long after she delivered."

I don't know what to say. Part of me feels like shit about blaming her for not being there to protect Brady. I also gave her shit daily because of her addiction, an addiction she wouldn't have had if she had not been raped and tormented by the memories of it daily. "Fuck me, this has been a shit couple of days. Crow, is Dane here yet? What the fuck is taking so long?"

I see him walking toward the door, talking on the phone. "They're at the gate now; Ghost is letting 'em in."

Fucking great.

Capone asks Melanie a question I've been wondering myself, "What the fuck is up with the Demons' road names? I mean, who the fuck just comes up with Asmodeus and Mammon? I have to know what the other names are, man, because that's just fucking weird." Leave it to Capone to make a room full of angry, nerved-up bikers laugh.

Melanie laughs as well, and explains, "They are the Demons MC, therefore, they have names that match their greatest sins. Asmodeus is a demon of Lust, and Mammon is one of Greed. All of the officers are named like that." She giggles.

Tats looks damn near enthralled with my baby sister.

"Tats, don't even think about it, asshole. She's my baby sister."

Tats throws his hands up and huffs, causing her to laugh again.

"I think I'll like it here just fine," she tells me before I send her with Navy and Bella to get cleaned up.

Once she's out of the room, Dane and Mike walk in.

"It's about damn time. I was starting to think you weren't coming. What do you have for me?"

Dane starts spouting off shit about locations and cell pings not too far from where we are now; fewer than three miles.

"Fuck yes, let's go get this motherfucker."

Johnny stops me with his hand on my shoulder. "I'm

going too, old man. Brady will stay here with Ghost and Navy, but I'm coming."

I'm already shaking my head as he's throwing on his jacket. "No way, Johnny. I can't risk you getting hurt. I can't lose you again, man. Please stay here with your brother."

"No can do, old-timer. I love you, Tank—like a father—but you will not take this chance away from me. I want this fucker gone. If you won't let me kill him myself, I at least want to witness his demise for all the pain he's caused us."

How the fuck can I deny him that? " Dammit! Fine, but you better fucking listen to me and stay close, got me?"

LAYLA

"Untie and strip her down, she's got to be thrown in that shower and washed up beforehand."

I can hear them talking, but am too weak to even open my eyes. I'm tired, so nauseous, and the wounds on my legs he's inflicted are more than likely infected. I can already feel the swelling in my face where he backhanded me repeatedly. All I can think about is someone finding me before they all rape me. Please God, let them find me.

TANK

"I t smells like shit out here, bro. What the hell is this place?" Johnny whisper-shouts.

"No, dude, that's not shit. It smells more like rotten pig and chicken guts. This must be an old slaughterhouse," Snoopy tells him without missing a beat.

"What the fuck? Do I want to know how you know what rotten pig guts smell like?"

Everyone yells, "hell no," at once. No one can stomach that fucking story again. Snoopy lived on a farm and some of his stories are fucking disturbing. It's turned some into vegetarians.

This place is not visible from the road, it's deep into the woods. The area must have been used as farmland a long time ago, the stench remains.

We took the cage because our bikes are too loud and the last thing we want to do is draw attention to our arrival.

After all, the boys love a surprise. I tell them to spread out, find an entrance, and wait for my signal.

We're ducked low and moving close to the wall of the slaughterhouse when the sound of laughter hits my ear. I stop, throwing my hand back to stop Johnny and put my finger to my lips then tap my finger to my ear for him to listen closely. He nods, letting me know he understands.

"Look at those big, full tits. I can't wait to bite those nipples and make this bitch scream. You good with that, Jamison?"

I jerk forward, but Johnny catches me and shakes his head.

"Hell yeah, you know I get off on watching that bitch in pain. I think I'll just sit back and watch you two fill her holes this time."

Johnny squeezes my shoulder and nods.

Whistling loud, giving my signal, we bust through the doors. "Surprise, surprise, motherfuckers." I point both pistols in their direction as Johnny holds an AR-15. "If I were you sick fucks, I would put your poor excuse for cocks back into your pants before they get shot the fuck off. I'm sure those whores you call wives wouldn't miss them, but you might."

Their hands fly up with the exception of Jamison. He sits in the corner, watching. His pants are undone as if he was going to enjoy his hand while watching these two bastards rape my ol' lady.

All of my brothers are in the room, as well as Mike and Dane. Memphis takes his shirt off and wraps it around Layla, taking her out of the building to the van.

"Well, Mike, it's so nice to see you again. How's that pretty little girl of yours?" Jamison taunts him, causing him to send a bullet zooming past his head.

"I missed on purpose, you sick fuck. I'm sure what these men have in mind for you will be much better than a bullet to the head, but . . ."

Pop. Pop. Pop. Pop. Both of the other officers hit the ground and I watch as their blood swirls around in the water before flowing down the drain.

"Damn, Mike, now I don't get to kill anybody and I was really looking forward to fucking some shit up tonight. You better start asking before you just begin popping motherfuckers. Damn." Capone pouts before leaving the room.

"You wanna make this quick, son, or do you wanna draw this shit out?"

The rest of the brothers exit as well, leaving me and Johnny alone with Jamison. He sits there with a smug look on his face as if he doesn't care he's about to die, which makes me want to drag him to our basement and chop his ass up.

"As bad as I would love to torture him the way he has my mom, brother, and me, I don't want to subject Brady to this man anymore. I think we should take care of him now."

I agree and know just the way to do it. I give Johnny my guns to hold then reach under the back of my vest and pull out the blade that started all of this in the first place. "Is this what you've been looking for all of these years, Byron? The blade I sliced Jeremy's body up with until he was unrecognizable."

His face turns red as anger takes over. "You son of a bitch, he was just a fucking kid." He jumps up, ready to attack, but Johnny shoves the AR-15 barrel to his forehead.

"Back the fuck up, Byron. You have no power here, asshole." He's right, he has absolutely no power over Johnny or anyone else anymore.

"Did Jeremy tell you he killed my little brother? Did he tell you he gave my thirteen-year-old brother, Brady, PCP? Fucking PCP! It caused him to have hallucinations of something inside of his body, so he took this blade and mutilated himself so badly that his body wouldn't even hold the damn embalming fluid.

"They had to wrap my baby brother in a fucking trash bag in order to hold the fluid in long enough for a funeral. I walked into a bloody-ass room only to hear him gurgle before taking his last breath at eight o'clock."

He's shaking his head as if what I'm saying could not be true.

"Oh, yeah. It's true, asshole. Every one of those little bastards laughed at the fact that my brother was tripping so hard off such a small hit, not caring one bit that Brady was dying while they were high off their asses. I did what I had to do to revenge my brother's death. I made sure all of them took their last breath at exactly eight o'clock, and what do you know, it's about that fucking time again."

He screams as I slice through his stomach repeatedly. I have no problem bathing in the blood of my fucking enemy as it squirts all over me and Johnny. "Anyone who hurts my family or my brothers will be sent to meet their maker."

His eyes are still wide as I bring the blade down, slicing

into his throat.

I look over at Johnny, making sure he's okay after everything he's just witnessed. His eyes are wide and his face is covered in blood.

"Are you okay, son? I'm sorry about all of the blood." I motion to his face and clothing, which are both drenched.

He shrugs nonchalantly while asking what we are going to do with the body.

Snoop walks back in, and says, "Johnny, why don't you go check on your mom? Memphis took her back to the clubhouse and his sister is taking care of her now. So you go ahead. Capone is waiting for you in the cage. Make sure to shower first, or you'll scare her to death."

He follows Snoop's directions without any problem, leaving us to discard the bodies.

"Come on, old man, there's a chicken pit out there, and trust me when I say, there's no better place to throw dead bodies than a fucking chicken pit."

I'm a southerner myself, but Snoop is on some hillbilly farmer type shit right now. "I'm a little scared to ask, but why is this pit so awesome for dead bodies?" I ask as we throw the tarp down and load the three bodies on it before rolling it up.

He grunts. "Because it is a very deep hole, dug for the sole purpose of guts, dead chickens, etcetera. They can be thrown in and burned without a second look."

So, that's exactly what we did.

LAYLA

My head feels groggy and I'm nauseous. I can hear people talking around me, but my eyes are too heavy to open.

"How long is she going to be asleep, Olivia?" I hear that deep, growly voice I love so much, but who the hell is Olivia?

"Don't you dare growl at me, asshole. I'm doing the best I can. She had an infection from the cuts on her legs, which caused her fever to rise pretty high. It's come down now, and I've done some blood work to make sure her count is back to normal. But that infection probably took its toll on her, making her extremely tired. The swelling in her face and around her eyes will come down in the next few days. You have to give her time, Tank."

I know he doesn't have one of his whores taking care of me. Lord, help him if he does because as soon as I'm able to move from this bed, I promise on all that is holy I will bust his damn head. I don't think I will ever get used to being around women he's slept with.

Gathering enough strength, I bring my hand up then back down hard onto the bed.

"Her heart rate is picking up. Layla? Layla, can you hear me? My name is Nurse Olivia. I'm Memphis' sister. You're safe now, and have nothing to be afraid of."

So she's a real nurse, Memphis' sister, not a whore. Thank God.

"That's odd, her heart rate is fine now. Maybe she was having a bad dream."

I hear Tank laugh at her assumption.

"If I was a betting man, I would say my little vixen here, is a bit jealous, or she thought you were interested in her man." The smug bastard. I can hear the grin practically splitting his face.

"Well, I don't want him, honey. Trust me. The Guardian Angels are beautiful, but not my cup of tea."

Tank's laughter fills the room once again. "Who wants tea when you can have Whiskey?" He kisses my hand before letting me know he'll be back soon to check on me, and that the boys want to visit for a while.

Brady's apologetic cry hurts my heart, but I can't get up enough energy to open my eyes. Why is it so hard?

"I'm so sorry, Mama. I know in my heart you would never intentionally hurt me. I know you did what you thought was best, and I've been such an asshole to you lately. I hope you can hear me, I love you."

After Brady pours his little heart out to me, Johnny does the same, letting me know it's over now and no one can hurt us anymore. "Byron Jamison is a dead man, Mama."

I have to push myself to get up so I can let them know it's not over just yet.

TANK

"Ihope you fellas don't mind my kids being in on this meeting, as it does involve them. We need to think about how we handle the cops if they come to our door with this bullshit. I'm almost positive that even though those three men were pieces of shit, someone is gonna come looking for them. If they do the research that we did, it's gonna send them straight to our neck of the woods." I look around at all of my brothers, my sons, Dane, and Mike, and thank God we all made it back this time, no losses. "Layla will be fine, though it may take a little while for the swelling to go down in her face. The gashes in her legs are deeper than we initially thought and will leave scars, but the antibiotics are clearing up the infection. He must have hit her with a rusty-ass, jagged pipe for infection to set in so soon. I just want to thank each and every person sitting at this table for helping save my ol' lady. It's one thing when we take on an enemy, but an enemy who's blue is a little riskier, and I'm damn proud to have all of you at my back."

Smiling faces and nods across the room make my heart fucking swell. I've worked hard to make sure we don't turn into straight savages, but when we have to be, it damn sure is nice to know all of the family is on board.

"Tank, Tank."

I hear Olivia outside the door and rush to see what's wrong.

"Look, I know you're in church and I hate bothering you, but as soon as you get done I need to see you." She turns to walk away.

I yell after her, "Olivia, is something wrong? Did you get the blood work back? Is she okay?" I'm popping off questions left and right, not giving her a chance to answer.

"Yes, the blood test came back, and there are a few things that need to be discussed as soon as you get a chance."

I adjourn the meeting, telling the boys I'm not sure they should come downstairs with me until I find out what's going on. They aren't happy but respect my wishes.

"What the hell is it, Olivia? Is something wrong with my shortcake?" Layla has always loved that nickname.

She put in a favor for a rush on the blood test. It's back way faster than I expected.

"It looks like her counts are coming back down to normal. I'll want to take another one in a few days to see where we stand with the infection. What I wanted to show you were her HGC levels, they are right around eight thousand."

She's looking at me as if I'm a fucking doctor, as though

I'm supposed to know what she's talking about. "You're pissing me off, Liv! I don't know what any of that shit means, and you're freaking me the fuck out." I'm pacing now, getting worried something is wrong with my girl. I just got her back, she has to be okay.

"Tank, calm your nasty-ass attitude down and stop fucking pacing. I'll dumb it down for you, you jerk. It means that Layla is about seven to eight weeks pregnant with your child."

I stop mid-pace, turning to look at a smiling Olivia. "What? Are you sure? That would mean . . . that would mean it happened on our first night together, again. Oh, shit, she's gonna kill me."

Olivia is laughing at me now. "I don't think she will kill you, but I do want to let you know a few things I will discuss with her as well when she's awake and feeling a little better. At her age, the risks are higher for quite a few things. Issues with hypertension, pre-eclampsia, gestational diabetes, and other things that could affect the baby."

I'm so lost, I don't know what any of those things are other than diabetes and hypertension and I only know of because my own doctors say I'm supposedly borderline.

"Tank, are you listening to what I'm saying to you?"

I nod and then tell her to go ahead and finish.

"Trust me, I am in no way trying to scare you. I only want to make you aware of everything that can happen, so you and Layla can discuss it. Now, as I was saying, there could be heart defects, abnormalities, and deformities. Down syndrome is a higher risk at this age, for example. That doesn't necessarily mean any of what I am saying will happen, but I'm warning you of what could. Okay?"

I need a drink or ten.

I tell her thanks, give my shortcake a kiss, then make my way upstairs to the bar. It's been a shit week and today is his birthday: March nineteenth. It never gets easier. With each year that passes it hurts just as much. I should have let him come with me that night and then none of this would have happened. But I didn't want to take the chance of him getting in trouble and being taken away from me.

I gulp down drink after drink until I have the courage to ride. There are two people I need to visit tonight. I sneak out through the back like I've done every year on this date since the Guardians took over this place.

"I bet you didn't expect to see me here tonight, did you? It's been a damn long time, Mama.

"I just wanted you to know that I now know the truth. I know why you were the way you were—what caused you to stay so medicated, so closed off from us boys, from life," my voice cracks. This is the night I always allow myself to let it out. "Thank you for giving me life, even though the night I was conceived, some vile bastard took yours. I'm sorry you had to endure so much pain that night, Mama, but I thank you for letting me live despite how I came about.

"I said a lot of bad things to you throughout the years, not knowing then all of the demons you faced daily. For that, I am so sorry. I know it doesn't mean anything now that you're not here, but I love you."

The tears won't stop falling from my face as I continue, "You have two handsome grandsons, and get this—their mother, my ol' lady, named one of them Brady. Without my permission, of course. She's as stubborn as they come. The other one is Johnny. They're both pretty damn great, but both have smart-ass mouths like their mother.

"I guess I can go ahead and tell you I have another one on the way, too, just found out a few hours ago." I hear a noise in the distance and turn only to see the trees blowing in the cold March breeze. "Well, I'm gonna walk on down to visit Brady now. I'll see you again next year. I love you, Mama."

Walking away, I feel somewhat lighter than before I came, like an old and heavy weight has been lifted. As Brady's grave comes into view, my eyes well with tears once more.

"Damn, B, it feels like forever since I've seen your happy, smiling face, man. I miss you more than you will ever know, little bro. I'll always blame myself for your death. I could have done something, anything different, and you would still be here with me. My right-hand man. Hell, you might have even had Snoop's spot as VP if you were here. But whatever you do, don't let him know I said that. He's a big guy, but sensitive. Damn, I miss you." The tears choke me up, but like always, I finish, "I know you didn't feel anything that night because of the phencyclidine but it still kills me to know you had so many gashes on your body. Why, brother? Why couldn't I get there in time?

"I will never forget walking into that room; the sound of your gurgling haunts my dreams. I don't even know if you heard me tell you I loved you before that last breath, and that eats at me. The guilt eats me alive, Brady."

A little red bird lands on Brady's tombstone, which is so

weird being as it's well after midnight and breezy out. It just sits there looking at me with its little head tilted as if waiting for me to finish my conversation.

"Well, B, it looks like you have a little friend tonight to keep you company, so I won't keep you long. I just wanted you to know that you were the best little brother I could have ever asked for and I pray one day you can forgive me and Mom for not being there for you that night. I found out Mom was fighting her own demons, which I'm sure you know now.

"You're an uncle to two wonderful boys and one more on the way. One of them carries your name. I sure wish you were here, little brother."

The little red bird flies onto my shoulder as if comforting me. I hear another sound that I know for a fact is not the trees whispering in the wind and turn around.

I see all of my officers, members, prospects, Navy, Olivia, Layla, and my boys. There's not a dry eye in the crowd.

"Since none of you respect my privacy, I guess come on over here and meet my little brother Brady. Layla, what are you doing out in this cold? I should blister your ass for this." I wrap her in close to me, trying to keep her warm as the boys and Navy introduce themselves.

"I see you have a friend." Navy points to the bird that will not leave my shoulder.

"Yeah, he just showed up and . . . never mind." I'm not about to tell them that this little thing is comforting, hell no.

Navy and Memphis share a knowing look before laughing, then Navy calls for Liam to come. Thie bird flies off of my shoulder and onto her hand. She coos at it, telling it she loves and misses him, and appreciates him letting us know Brady was okay.

"I—I don't understand, Navy. What the hell is this about?" I'm sure I look confused as hell.

"Before Liam died, he told me that anytime I needed him or missed him to just look for the red birds. He said he would always be around. I'm sure this is his way of letting you know Brady is okay and that he loves you and does not blame you for what happened."

I can't help or stop the tears that begin falling again. Layla and my boys comfort me.

As I walk back toward my bike—them back to the cage—Johnny yells out to me, "Don't think I didn't hear you say y'all was having another baby, old man. We will discuss this in the basement, inside the ring."

I throw my head back with laughter. "You got it, son."

LAYLA

It's been two days since I found out I was pregnant and watched the man I love pour his heart out at his mother's and brother's grave. I know I need to talk to him about the other women who need to be saved, but I want to give him time. He just found out he has a sister, that he's a product of rape, and his mother was hurt physically on that night and suffered mentally every day after. He's not saying much, but I know he's having a hard time dealing with everything.

"Hey, girly, how ya feeling?" Navy walks over to me, holding a beautiful Bella.

"I'm feeling better, thank you. My face and legs still hurt, but since the swelling has gone down, I feel much better."

She smiles at me. "That's awesome, but how do you feel about having another baby?"

Ah, yes, the baby. "I have to admit, I was shocked at

first to find out that after all of these years I was going to experience pregnancy again. But if I'm being honest, I'm pretty excited about it." I know that's something else Tank is worried about: the risks are much higher at my age.

"Hi, Layla. I haven't had the opportunity to introduce myself with everything that's gone on. I'm Melanie, Tank's sister."

I pull her into a big hug. "It's so good to meet you. Byron kept saying he had Tank's sister hanging in a warehouse, and I was so afraid he had already hurt you."

Her eyes water as if she's never had anyone worry or care for her before. "Thank you. He did hurt me, along with many others, before putting me into that cage. I can't imagine the pain I would have endured had the Guardians not found me. Only God knows what he would have done to you if they hadn't shown up when they did. His hate for Zane is beyond anything I've ever seen. He's a man of pure evil, a demon through and through." It's like she's lost inside her head right now, remembering the evil she's seen.

"I have something to ask you, but it needs to stay between us for now, until Tank has a little time to himself. Navy, this goes for you too, no talking to Memphis until I talk to Tank."

They both give me their attention and nod in agreement.

"Have you heard anything about women being held against their will, being raped and sold off like pieces of fucking meat?"

Her eyes tell me everything I need to know.

"How many, Melanie? Do you remember?"

She shakes her head. "I don't know how many, but I do

know they are young. A couple of them can't be older than ten."

My breath catches. "Are you kidding me? Fucking ten years old? That's a baby! A fucking baby! How could he do this?" I'm off of my stool and on my way to find Tank before she can say anymore.

How could I be with a man who rapes children? I'm disgusted. I only get as far as opening the door and stepping outside before retching off of the porch.

"Layla!" I hear boots crunching against the gravel and then my hair is being pulled back and a warm hand rubs circles on my back. "Baby, are you okay? What's wrong? I know you're having sickness because of the pregnancy, but the look on your face when you opened the door said something totally different."

I rise and wipe my mouth, looking into his concerned eyes. "You noticed my facial expression from way over there, old man?"

His laugh is beautiful and one of the many things I've missed about him all of these years. "Okay. So, you've got jokes. But yes, shortcake, I notice everything about you. Now cut the shit and tell me what's going on." He still knows me well, even over a damn decade and a half.

"Um, do you want to sit down first?"

He crosses his big arms, causing those delicious muscles to bulge. "Dammit, Layla, stop fucking around. Pregnancy or not, you can and will get that little ass spanked. Do *you* need to sit down? If not, spit it out!"

I stomp over to the bench and sit. "While he had me in there, I overheard some things. I wanted to give you some time to gather your thoughts and get your head around everything that's been going on, but now that I know a little more information, I can't just sit on it. I knew that precinct was corrupt, but I never imagined anything like this. The Lieutenant made those two men with Byron take more girls to a different location. He thought Melanie would tell you the original location. They have girls as young as ten years old, baby. Ten! These are babies, Zane. We have to save them. Someone is supposed to be contacting Byron about buying in two days. They're hanging in some damn restaurant somewhere."

"Fuck, Layla! You should have told me as soon as you opened your eyes, baby. Never delay on shit like this, no matter what I'm going through. Fucking ten years old! Fucking shit!" He kicks over the large trash can, causing a loud crash that brings all the brothers to us.

The anger radiating from their president pulls them toward us.

"It's bad, fellas," Tank tells them. "We need a plan and a man on the inside. Call Dane and tell him to get Mike's ass over here, now!"

TANK

"I'll never understand hurting innocent women, but little girls—that's just fucking sick. It's downright motherfucking disturbing! We need a plan, like, yesterday. I want these bastards gone, but that Lieutenant—a man who is supposed to protect at all cost, make sure his officers are in line and doing right by each and every law-abiding citizen; he is mine."

He thinks it's okay to rape kids and sell them. I'm gonna show him what it feels like for an unwilling hole to be breached. I need all of the stuff ready downstairs, every object imaginable that can be used to rape his ass before I cut off and feed him his own fucking cock.

"Where the fuck is—"

My door slams.

"We're right here, asshole. Stop yelling. What the fuck is going on now?" Dane yells.

I give all the fellas, including Mike and Dane, the rundown. Mike confirms it, then tells us that it has been going on for a long time now, but he never knew the location.

"So, what's the plan? How do we find out where they are?" Mike asks the question we all want to know.

"That's what we gotta figure out. Layla said it's in the bottom of a restaurant—the Lieutenant's wife's restaurant."

Mike is out of his seat, hands hitting the table. "Why didn't you say that to start with! That bitch has a little hole-in-the-wall Italian restaurant off of old one twenty-nine. Horrible fucking food, but a good location to hide women and kids, I guess. Its entire downstairs is completely soundproof. Why did I not think of that shit before? Sneaky son of a bitch." He's as amped as we are about taking down these fucking pedophiles.

"We've got two days, then the buyers reach out to Byron. Now, I'm positive he won't be answering but just as positive that the Lieutenant will. So, we need a plan, now."

Snoop speaks up for the first time tonight, "I guess it's a good thing I have his phone then, isn't it?" He tosses the phone in my direction.

"You sneaky-ass motherfucker. When did you even have time to get that shit?"

He shrugs. "Right before we tossed him, it fell out. I thought it might come in handy. And well, here you are, Prez, all needy and shit."

My shoulders shake in silent laughter before flipping him the finger. "It is definitely needed, asshole. We can keep up with how much time we have left depending on when these predators make contact. Tonight I need everybody's brain working overtime. Come sunrise, I need a concrete plan that won't blow smoke in the Guardians' direction, got me?

"Now, I'm going to spend some time with my kids and my woman before having blood on my hands tomorrow. We good? Any questions?"

Capone raises his finger. "I just need to know what you and Memphis have been drinking lately."

Everyone looks as confused as I am.

"I need to know, so I don't drink that shit because I'm just not ready to become a pussy-whipped motherfucker like you two." His face is serious.

Cackles fill the room as I yell for them all to get the fuck out. I can't wait for that little shit to get hit with the love bug. Fuck, maybe I am a little bitch now—*love bug*, really? I shake my head all the way to my room.

As I'm pushing the door open, Byron's phone rings. I hesitate. I'm not sure if I should answer or not, being as they aren't supposed to reach out until tomorrow. The ringing stops only to start back up a moment later. Dammit.

"Hello." I hear nothing. "Speak, motherfucker."

"It seems you have something that belongs to me, Tank. Something I've rather enjoyed playing with all night, and I now have something that belongs to you."

A barking chorus of laughter echoes in my ears before I hear him scream, "Dad!"

The phone falls from my hand at the same time my heart falls from my chest. Brady's first time calling me *dad* comes at a time when he is being kidnapped and possibly tortured. A sound of pure agony rips from my chest, bringing every

Guardian Angel rushing.

I look behind me, my eyes automatically connect with Layla's. I can't hide my fear on this, and she sees it loud and fucking clear.

She shakes her head. "What happened, Zane?"

I look behind her at Johnny.

"What the fuck happened, Zane?" Her head swivels around the room. "No. No! Where's Brady? Where's my baby, Tank?" She takes off, no doubt looking for him.

"Navy, please try to calm her down so she doesn't hurt herself or the baby. They have Brady and we aren't waiting until morning, we're riding tonight. Fuck a plan. They wanna fuck with a son of a fucking Guardian Angel? No. We don't need a plan, we go in guns fucking blazing."

LAYLA

O h my God, my baby boy. I don't know what I've done in this life to disappoint you, God, but please give me a chance to fix it. Please, don't take my baby away from me. I need him here. What if I have a girl this time? Johnny will need help beating the shit out of anyone who tries to hurt her. So, you see, he is needed here.

"Layla, you need to calm down before you hurt yourself or the baby, sweetheart. I know it's scary not knowing what's going to happen, but—"

I don't want to hear this shit and tell her so, "Navy, you do not have a clue how I feel, so please spare me the calm-down bullshit."

Apparently, I'm not the only hot-headed one in the room now.

"You don't know shit about me, you uppity bitch. I sat watching my sweet little boy waste away to nothing from fucking cancer, large tumors that destroyed his tiny body. I stayed scared and uncertain from the first time he was diagnosed until the day I watched him take his last breath. So the next time you wanna assume you know something about someone, you better check your shit first. That's a good way to get on my shit list.

"Now, sit your ass down somewhere and relax, trust that your man knows what the fuck he's doing because he does. He will bring your boy home. I'm calling my damn mama to cook us something good to eat."

She's still talking, mumbling under her breath as she stomps across the room, but I hear her words, "I've chopped a bitch into pieces without blinking, thinking she was my mother for twenty-plus years. This bitch must not know I will cut her. No one yells at me.

"Hey, Mama," she hisses into the phone.

What in the hell have I done? Now I've pissed off the only other *ol' lady* here. I may have to sleep with one eye open for a while. I feel like shit for not knowing details of her son's illness and his battle—their battle. If I learned anything, it's that when someone you love suffers, so do you. I'll apologize after she calms down.

I watch her sling shit around the room as she yells at her mom to hurry her ass up and make us lasagna. Yep, definitely after she calms down.

TANK

Riding usually calms me, but not this time. I'm fueled by fucking rage and nothing, no one can extinguish the fire burning within me.

We are looking for some Italian restaurant in this raggedy-ass town called Francesca's. Apparently, it's authentic and extremely expensive, so the only traffic it gets is from high society folk. Yeah, fucking right.

Memphis throws his left hand up, letting us know it's coming up on our left. It doesn't take long to spot the one and only restaurant in this area that looks more like a fucking bed 'n' breakfast—dainty, white lights hang in what looks to be a patio area, giving the place an elegant type of look. We pull into the gravel parking lot. Yep, fucking gravel—all of the money these motherfuckers are getting yet they can't shell out to pave the parking lot. Dust flies around us as our bikes come rumbling to a stop out front. I cant wait to see the looks on these fuckers faces when they realize we prefer the in-your-fucking-face approach.

A bell rings above our heads as we walk inside, alerting them that they have customers. An older Italian lady approaches, her smile falters as soon as she sees us. Capone takes the lead before I even know what's happening.

With an evil smile on his face, he says, "*Ciao Cagna*."

She gasps, throwing her hand to her chest like he has insulted her. "*Tu chi sei?*"

He throws his head back and laughs before looking her in her eyes with an expression I've never seen him wear. "*Il tuo peggior fottuto incubo cagna*."

I need to learn some Italian.

"Why do you come into my restaurant and call me a bitch? What is it that you want from me?"

I take it upon myself to answer her question, "We want you to change your fucking menu, you sick fucks. Where is your husband?"

Her downcast eyes let me know the answer.

We start walking toward the stairs, but she steps in front of us.

"Bitch, please don't make me shoot you. With or without your cooperation we are going into that basement. Tats, go take care of the few sick fucks in here looking to buy."

She goes to stop him, but Capone puts a bullet in her skull. Thankfully, he'd put a silencer on.

"Damn, Pone, you're getting pretty violent, dude. Are you not having enough sex?"

He gives me a "Fuck you" before moving for the stairs.

It's almost as if we have to go into an underground

tunnel. After getting to the bottom of the stairs there's a long-ass hallway leading to a door. Halfway to the door, we hear the screams of a little girl: "No! Please don't hurt me! Just let me go home to my mama and daddy! Please!" I can hear her chains rattle as she tries to break free. I'm sick.

"You leave her alone, you fucking piece of shit. You wanna fuck with somebody, why don't you fuck with someone who's not a fucking child, you sick fucking pervert." Brady, oh fuck. My boy is trying to piss them off and distract them. Keep it up, B, Dad is on the fucking way.

I stand at the door, listening for when we need to go in.

"Shut your mouth, you little shit, or I'll shut it for you, and not in a way you'll enjoy, pretty boy. You ever had your mouth raped?"

I hear laughter around the room. There are more than a couple of them.

"Yeah, boss, let's play. The little one over there just laid around like a dead fish; didn't get me off properly. Maybe this one will be fun."

That's it, I can't take it anymore. We bust in the door, guns raised and ready to fire at anything that fucking moves.

"Well, well, well. I'm assuming you brought my little Melanie back to me in order to get this little loud-mouthed fucker back. At least Melanie knew to be quiet as she took my cock."

Tats lurches forward, grabbing him by the throat, and holds him against the wall. "Which one of you was talking before we came in the room—something about a dead fish?"

I look around, observing every face in this room until one in particular won't meet my eyes. I look at his uniform.

"Rogers, is it?" I motion with my head for Crow to tie his ass up and get him in the cage.

"All of you sick fucks are going to die tonight, but your willingness to answer my questions, and the answers you give, will determine how fast that death will be. Fuck with me or don't answer my questions, and you will receive the same torturous rape and murder both of those men are guaranteed. Understood? Throw all of your guns down and kick that shit over. Now." If it's one thing I hate, it's a child molester, a fucking pedophile rapist.

I cut my son the rest of the way down, and make sure he's okay. "Did anyone touch you, son?" I whisper close, so I don't embarrass him.

He shakes his head as tears fall. "No, Dad, but—" He looks over to the other cage at a small girl curled up into a ball.

"Son?"

He ignores me and walks to the cage, then yells, "Go outside and get the keys from that sick fuck, Memphis."

He's back in no time, giving Brady the keys. Every man in this room who's not a Guardian is in cuffs and will die tonight. Rage is all I feel as I watch my son unlock the cage and pull that little girl out.

He cradles her in his arms like a baby and walks my way. "I'm taking her with me, Dad, so she can have a proper burial."

What the fuck! "Son, what do you mean? A burial? She's dead?"

Tears fall from his eyes as he nods then walks out of the room, taking what can only be a girl of about thirteen years of age outside to the cage.

Capone wastes no time killing every motherfucker in the room as he screams out in anger. We walk through curtains that were obviously put up to separate the rooms. On the other side is a sight no one should ever see.

Twenty-plus girls hang in cages, as well as five boys, most of them barely clothed, some have been brutally beaten. Thank God we brought two cages this trip. We're gonna need them both.

"We won't hurt any of you, okay? We're going to get you down and get you all back home with your families," Tank says softly.

We take each one down, and when I come to a little girl who's about ten, she smiles at me. "Are you Brady's daddy?"

Her sweet voice and smile make me smile even though I'm far from happy. "Yes, princess, I most certainly am Brady's dad. Who are you?"

Her smile widens, lighting up her whole face. "My name is Haleigh James. Brady said you would save us, that you wouldn't give up until you found us. Thank you, mister." She jumps into my arms, hugging me tightly.

I look over at Capone to see him wipe his eye before turning away. Yeah, me too brother, me too.

After leaving nothing but smoke and flames on old 129, we ride.

On my ride home, I could only think of these kids and the hell I'm sure they've been through. The devastation on my boy's face nearly brought me to my knees, and I'm not sure at this point how he will get past what I'm sure was a fucking horrific act he had to witness. I want to comfort him and make him talk about what he saw, but at the same time, I don't want him relieving that fucking nightmare.

As soon as we're home I'll get some of the prospects to dig a nice burial spot, so we can have a nice family gathering and a going-home celebration for that beautiful little soul taken away by those vile fucks. Tomorrow I'll have Navy, Layla, and Queenie cook a nice meal, have a couple of the brothers get a tombstone made, as well as a casket and some flowers. My son wants a respectful burial for her, so she will damn well get the best one I can possibly give, without involving anyone who will ask too many questions. We don't even know her name, only that she was thirteen.

I wish we could have done more than a bullet to the head for these sick bastards. Unfortunately, we didn't have enough room to bring them all back to be tortured, but oh, how the other two will be tortured in the worst of ways. I can't fucking wait.

LAYLA

I'm pacing, eating another plate of the lasagna Queenie will be giving me the recipe to when I see headlights at the gate. It doesn't take long for both vans to come through, followed by the bikes.

"Navy! Navy, they're here!" I yell.

She, her parents, and Melanie come running out of the kitchen. Olivia runs after them. Memphis must have called her. Someone must be hurt.

"Please let everyone be okay," as soon as the words leave my mouth, Brady walks through the door. His face is bruised, tear-stained and though that worries me terribly, it's not my biggest concern.

He has a beautiful little blonde girl cradled to his chest as if he has to keep her near to protect her.

"Brady, baby."

He whispers that he loves me, but walks straight past me to the couch. Instead of laying her down as I expected, he sits down with her still wrapped tightly in his arms. It's a heartbreaking sight.

"Brady, honey, why don't you let me take her and get her fed and washed up."

Tank gives a quick shake of his head, confusing me as to why I shouldn't help. Turning back to see the turmoil in my son's eyes, I realize that was not the right thing to say.

"She's dead, Mama. Fucking dead, and I couldn't do anything to stop it! Nothing. You can't feed her, but washing all of their filth off of her body and finding her a pretty blue dress to be buried in would be nice."

Oh, how my heart is in pieces right now for this little girl, for her family, and my son. I can't express the sorrow I feel.

The door creaks open and I turn, shocked at all of the girls and boys who were saved from what I would only consider to be hell. I never would have imagined so many were there, in fucking cages, like animals.

"Take them all downstairs. Olivia and Jacob will look them over, give medical care if needed," Tank yells across the room.

Every brother, with the exception of Memphis and Crow, help the kids downstairs.

Olivia approaches Brady then squats down in front of him. "I'm proud of you, young man. It takes a lot to endure what you did, see what you had to see, and still put this young lady first. Do you think I could take her downstairs and clean her up a bit?"

Olivia reaches for her, but he pulls back.

"I promise you, Brady, she is in good hands with me.

She won't be hurt anymore."

I'm in tears as water gathers at the corners of my baby's eyes. He finally releases her into Olivia's arms. "You did good, son."

He looks at me and I don't know what, but something changes in my son, in this moment. "I'm going to take a shower, Mama," is all he says before disappearing down the hallway.

TANK

"This is going to be so fun, so fucking fun. I won't get to enjoy it as much as I should, though because at the end of the day, there's still a little girl dead and many others tortured. No amount of torture will take that back, and it damn sure won't take the devastation out of my son's eyes," I say to no one in particular as we all stand around these two disgustingly pitiful excuses for men.

They are strapped face-down and naked to the tables in the middle of our basement. "Johnny, did you get me the Vaseline and gloves I asked for?"

He smiles. "Yeah, old man, I got 'em. I brought a few extra items, too, that Navy told me to give to you. She said you better use 'em or she would find out and have to cut you."

What the fuck is with that psycho and cutting? "Okay. Where is it?"

He laughs, pointing to the table where he not only placed the Vaseline and gloves, but the biggest purple dildo I have ever seen.

"The fuck is wrong with your girl, Memphis? That thing is huge. I hope you don't go in behind that damn thing, you'd drown."

He smirks and throws the vibrant dildo at me. "Nah, my cock's bigger."

Snoopy scoffs. "Dude, your shit ain't even half the size of that thing. No fucking way."

I shake my head at these crazy assholes. "Either way, it's getting used on these fucks tonight. Let's get started. Oh, and I've decided against the lube. I'm sure you filthy motherfuckers didn't use any." I shove the dildo deep inside of the Lieutenant, all the way to the base, and listen to him scream through the duct tape over his mouth.

Rogers is squirming beside him, clenching his ass.

"Don't worry, Rogers, you're next. You'll be a dead fish by the time we're done with you, motherfucker," I say before yelling at Capone, "Yo, Capone, what else do we have over there?"

He walks over, grabbing a blade and a huge-ass butt plug. He hands me the plug and I immediately give him a what-the-fuck look. "My sis said to use it, so use it. I'll use this." He holds up a jagged blade as he approaches the Lieutenant.

Jerking out the dildo, he replaces it with the knife, plunging it in over and over again. The jagged edges cut through his flesh, causing large amounts of blood, mucus, and shit to discharge from his ass. His cries and wrenching to get loose do nothing to deter Capone or his rage. He rips the knife down, cutting his cock and balls off in one quick motion.

The only screams now come from the man who killed that little girl, he knows his fate is sealed.

"Tank! Ta—oh my God!" Layla pukes all over the place.

"Damn, baby, you know you can't be down here while club business is going on. Are you okay? What's wrong?"

She points up the stairs before speaking, "It's Brady, he won't come out of the bathroom. I heard glass break."

I tell the boys to make me proud and send Navy down to help them destroy every hole he has. I enjoy his screams before closing the door.

I run down the hallway, stopping right outside the bathroom door where I can hear my son sobbing like a baby, and my heart breaks. "Son, are you okay in there? Your mom said she heard something break."

He doesn't answer, only continues to sob.

"Brady?"

The lock clicks, so I gently push the door open to see my son on the floor of the shower still fully clothed. He's soaking wet, with blood washing down the drain where he punched his hand through the glass door of the shower.

"I couldn't stop them, Dad. I couldn't save her. I tried so hard to get my hands loose, but I just couldn't."

It's then that I notice all of the red welts around his wrists. "Damn, son, I'm so sorry. I don't know what you witnessed, but I do know how witnessing something tragic can affect you, and your whole life. Don't do what I did, Brady. Don't go half of your life without getting it off of your chest. If I'm not that person or you're just not ready, you have a huge family who has your back. When you are ready to talk, we'll be here. Don't hesitate. And whatever you do, don't let the guilt you feel fester. That in itself will send you into an early grave. You are not to blame, your hands were tied, too, son." I pull him in for the first time, hugging him as tight as I can. But I know those broken pieces take time to find their proper places again.

* * *

Brady informed me last night that he wanted the name *Blue* written on her tombstone. Of course, he didn't go into detail as I wished he would, but I made sure to tell the boys to make it happen. As we stand here today, laying this beautiful girl to rest, I watch my son—a son I hadn't known existed until a few months ago. I couldn't imagine losing him, not having answers to his whereabouts or his demise. I would go to the ends of the earth to find those answers, as I'm sure Blue's parents have been doing.

Dane and Mike have been working together with the Missing Persons Unit, looking to find any photos resembling the younger kids who didn't know their addresses. Some were not even from Georgia. These assholes have people in almost every state taking these kids. I will do everything I can to find those fucks and make sure they meet their maker.

"Dad, can I say something before they lower the casket?"

I nod and watch as my son walks over then crouches down beside her at her final resting place. "I'm so sorry,

Blue. I'll always carry you with me. In my heart, you will always be. You were so young, so beautiful, and did not deserve what happened to you. If I could have taken your place, sweet girl, I would have. If I could have saved us both, I would have. I'm going to make it my mission in life to take down any motherfucker who hurts kids. I'm sorry," his voice breaks, and his brothers, all of them, surround him. They throw in the blue flowers as they lower her into the ground.

As soon as we're back at the clubhouse, which didn't take long because we buried her on our land along with some damn good men we've lost along the way, we sit down to eat. I'm about to tell Brady some news I've been wanting to share with him but my phone rings.

"Yeah? Wait—I thought you said it would take a while to find them. No, no, it's fine. Come on through." Damn, I wish I had known it was gonna be this fast, we could have waited to bury her. "Brady, I was just about to tell you something I consider to be good news, but I don't have time to explain now, let's go."

Every single person follows us into the main room. I stand with my arm around Brady's shoulders as Dane walks in, followed by a couple who look to be around thirty-five.

I hear my son's intake of breath before he jerks out of my hold. "How could you do this, Dad? How could you hurt them this way? Her—me—how . . . Why?" He's crying so hard he can't finish a whole sentence. He takes off to the room he'd been sleeping in.

I'm lost and don't understand where I went wrong. How the hell does he even know who they are? I look over and the answer to my question is staring right at me: the palest blue eyes filled with grief and pain. This is why he wanted *Blue* on her tombstone. Fuck.

"Is it okay with you, Mister Tank, if I talk to your son?"

I tell her I don't mind if his mother doesn't, then point to a very upset Layla. "Come on, I'll take you to him. But, please, don't make him relive anything. As you can see, he's having a very hard time dealing with everything."

Layla walks her back to talk to our son and for some reason, I feel like she's not gonna get the answers she came for. He's not ready, and honestly, I don't know if he ever will be.

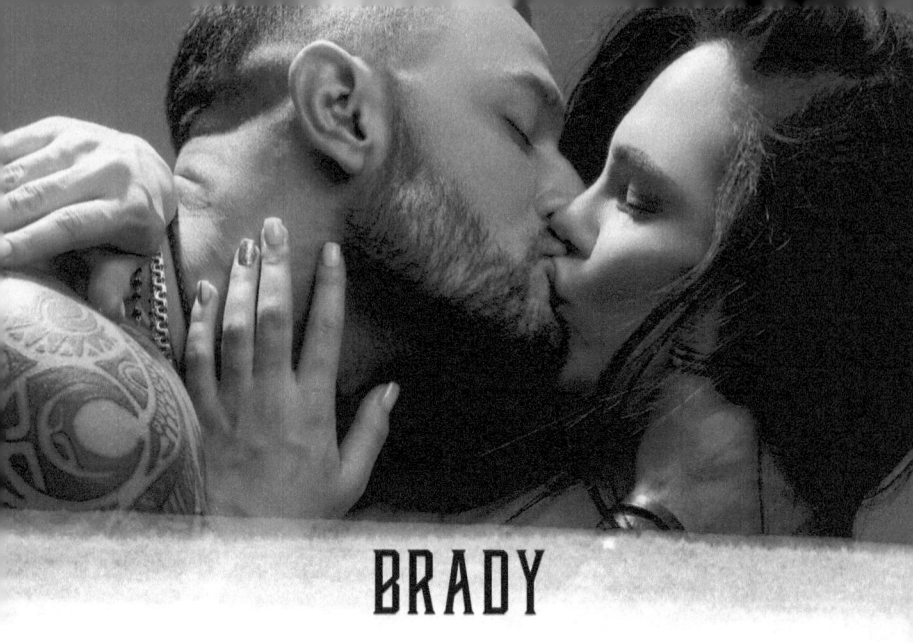

BRADY

"**B**rady, baby, Mrs. Holloway would like to speak to you for just a few moments, if that's okay. No pressure, she promised."

I tell Mom to let her in. She's pale-skinned with white hair and the bluest eyes. Everybody kept saying blonde hair, but it's white just like her daughter's.

"She looked just like you. I've never seen eyes so pale blue before. They're beautiful."

Tears fall from her eyes as she comes to sit by me on the bed. "So, it's true, it was my little Kennedy. She—well, I have a rare form of ocular albinism and passed it on to our children. That's why they're so blue. She's been missing for about three months now. We've looked everywhere from North to South Georgia, drained our bank accounts following lead after lead only to be disappointed. Every. Single. Time. This time though, when Dane came to my door, I prayed he was wrong, that it was just another bullshit lead. That's not the case though, is it?"

I shake my head. "I won't tell you what happened—not because you don't deserve the truth, but because you wouldn't want to hear those things, and I can't relive it right now. You know where this place is. I will give you my dad's number if you decide, later on down the line, when all of this isn't so fresh for us, that you still want to know. I will tell you, Mrs. Holloway. I will tell you every single detail. Right now, just know that your beautiful daughter was brave, a fighter. I was in the room with her, talking to her the whole time. She didn't die alone."

Her tears hit my hand, which she's holding. "Thank you, Brady. Thank you for bringing her with you and giving her a resting place." She gets up to leave, but I stop her.

"One last thing, ma'am. I didn't know her name to have it put on her stone, so it just says *Blue*. If you want to have it changed, I am okay with that. Kennedy is a pretty name."

She walks back and puts one hand on my cheek. "You sweet, sweet, boy. That is beautiful, and she would have loved it. It is very fitting, don't you think?" She gives me a quick peck on the cheek then she's out the door.

I'll never get past those eyes and the pain they held, both Kennedy's and her mother's.

LAYLA

"Tank, I'm so worried about Brady. He hasn't come out of that room in days. Do you think he will be okay? Will he ever get past this?" I'm rambling, it's what I do when I'm nervous or upset. I hate seeing my son in pain, especially when I don't have the slightest clue how to fix it for him.

"Babe, between all of the shit Byron put you all through and what he witnessed in those cages, it's enough to drive a grown man to murder. I can't imagine what or how his teenage brain is processing everything right now. He feels rage, I'm certain. I see it in him and, that, I think he's okay with. It's the others he's trying to figure out. We have to let him deal with it in his own way, and be there to catch him if he falls."

I snuggle in close, breathing in Zane's smell. It comforts me when my emotions are all over the place.

He rubs his hand across my belly and kisses me. "You have to stop stressing, shortcake. It's not good on you or jellybean."

I laugh at his cute nickname for the baby. "Jellybean—that's cute."

He kisses down my neck to my collarbone. We haven't had sex in days because I've been so worried, but my libido is off the charts since becoming pregnant again.

"Is this okay, Layla?" He licks each nipple, sucking and biting, which gets me going.

"Yes, yes it's fine. Don't stop . . . ever."

I hear him chuckle as he dips his tongue inside my bellybutton. "Is someone feeling neglected and needy tonight?"

I growl when he stops to look up at me.

"Oh, I think I'm gonna love you being pregnant, babe. So needy and dirty for me. Mm." He flattens his tongue and takes one long lick up my wet core.

My body is overheated, and I feel like I'm going to come out of my skin if I don't get what I need right now. "Please, Tank. I need you. Now!"

He jerks my legs apart before burying his face in my pussy. He eats me like a man starving. I force myself up into his face and mouth, afraid I won't get enough of him. I don't remember feeling this way, this needy during my first or second pregnancies. Maybe it's because I'm with the man I love—the man who's always had my heart.

"I need you, Zane."

He crawls over me, settling in between my thighs. I feel him, hot and heavy at my entrance. He peppers my face with soft kisses. The anticipation is killing me, so I reach between us, grabbing his shaft and guiding him inside me.

"Are you happy, shortcake? Does your greedy pussy feel nice and full now?"

I roll my hips, trying to get some friction, causing him to laugh louder this time. "I would be happier if you would stop teasing me and move. You've seen me angry. Trust me, you do not want to see me pregnant and angry," I snarl at him, but it works, because now he's moving, slowly, but moving.

Every roll of his hips, as he grinds inside of me, lights me on fire. I can feel him against every wall. "Zane. Yes," I chant, as I come. He picks up speed, which prolongs my orgasm. My back comes up off of the bed as he wraps those big arms around me, pulling me up and into his lap. I bounce up and down while he bites and sucks on my neck. I'm sure I'll have marks tomorrow, but I'm not sure I care. "Oh, Zane, baby. I'm about to come again."

"That's it, baby, give me all of it."

I throw my head back as I come. A moan escapes my parted lips and I'm sure I'm loud enough to be heard by everyone within a hundred feet, but I don't care. His body jerks as he comes, and he bites down on my neck with a growl.

TANK

Six-and-a-half months later

I'm so tired of my two kids being assholes. Enough is enough. "Layla! Layla, baby! Come get your damn kids!" I turn to see her, Melanie, and Navy coming out of the kitchen.

She waddles over with another damn pickle. "Will you stop all of that damn yelling, Tank. You can't act like a child every time you get your ass beat at pool. Honey, I'm sorry, but you're just not that good. Maybe you should try something else. Foosball or something," she says with her mouth full.

I'm fucking baffled. I look around at all of my brothers, my sister, and kids, to see them all trying to hide their snickering.

"Excuse the fuck out of me, Layla, but your kids are fucking cheats, first of all. And never suggest I play Foosball again, it ain't gonna happen, babe. Fucking *ever*! Got me? The last time I checked, I was the president of the Guardian Angels and a bad motherfucker at that, so all of you standing around laughing, just remember that when shit detail comes up. Y'all assholes will be stuck doing it. Especially you prospects." I point to Ghost and Johnny, causing their shit-eating grins to fall from their faces.

"Dad, just admit you lost. I beat your ass fair and square, man. So did Johnny. You scratch on the eight ball, you lose. It's just that simple, old man. Now pay up—I want my hundred bucks. Next time, I'm coming for that roadrunner out back." The gall of this kid, my fucking kid.

"Hell no, kid. No one gets the roadrunner. It's a fucking classic. I know you've got your license now, but you'll start off in some cheap piece of shit to learn. Even after that, you'll never sit behind the driver seat of my car."

He smiles, as does everybody in the room like they know something I don't.

Oh, fuck no. I point at him. "You little shit, you better not have been in my car already. If I go out there and that seat has been tampered with, moved even an inch, I will bend you over my damn knee and bust your ass, Brady."

Brady's been doing a little better lately, but he's still not himself. He uses humor to hide his pain.

"Um, Tank," Layla tries to talk, but I cut her off because she's not going to defend this little shit if he's been in my car.

"Not now, Layla. This is serious shit we're discussing. Right now is not the time to baby him. We are talking about my baby, my fully restored sixty-nine roadrunner, with a four forty V-eight engine six-pack. It is fucking immaculate."

"No, you asshole! I'm talking about *your baby*—my water just broke!"

Holy shit, I'm gonna be a dad. I mean, I'm already a dad, but fuck, oh fuck. "Okay. Nobody panic. Melanie, grab the bags. Crow, grab the cage. I'll grab Layla. Let's roll. A new Guardian Angel is coming into the world today."

"Wait, baby. Can you grab my pickle, please?"

If she wasn't dead-ass serious I would cuss her out right now.

"Dammit, Johnny, grab your mom's pickle. Fuck it, bring the whole damn jar just in case!" I don't know what to do. I've never done this before. Shit, I'm so nervous.

All of my brothers and family are outside in the waiting area, only I was allowed in.

"How are you feeling, baby, you need anything?" I squeeze her hand lightly, letting her know I'm here.

The hospital staff put her on some kind of medicine to keep her from having seizures because her blood pressure kept rising, but the medicine has made her sick.

"Ice cubes were all the nurse said I could have in case they have to do surgery."

Why the hell would they have to do surgery? I'm glad this is our last child because I'm not sure my nerves could handle watching her sick like this again.

"Okay. Are we ready yet? I'm going to check to see where we're—oh, never mind. We are ready. I can feel the baby right here. Are you ready to push, Layla? On the count of three, I'm gonna need a big push, okay?"

Layla nods and waits for three. She squeezes my hand,

bears down, and pushes. Her screams are agonizing, and can probably be heard outside in the waiting room. I wouldn't be surprised if the door gets broken down at any minute by one of my brothers.

The doctor tells her he needs another big push, and she's a rockstar, doing just that.

"Zane, it feels like it's ripping my vagina apart! How does it look?" My eyes go wide as she begins to yell, "You did the shit to me! The least you can do is tell me if my vagina is still intact, you inconsiderate piece of donkey ass—oh my God!"

Cries and screams fill the room as my baby finally makes an entrance into this world.

"Congratulations! It's a girl."

I'm in awe as I watch them clean my little girl. She's eight pounds and healthy, with all of her fingers and toes. "Our family is complete now, baby. We have our two handsome boys and a beautiful little girl."

They hand my daughter to her mother, and I watch as she looks up at me with wonder in her eyes. "Hi, beautiful girl, I'm your daddy."

"She looks just like you, Zane. She's beautiful. I know you thought it was a boy, but did you at least pick one name in case it was a girl?" I didn't, so I throw her another idea, "How about we let her brothers name her? Would that be okay?"

She smiles. "That would be perfect."

LAYLA

It's been one whole month since we brought home Kennadi Storm Porter, and let me tell you, she is a feisty little thing already. Don't be five minutes late on a feeding, because she will make you regret it. But when she's asleep in my arms, like she is right now, looking just like her father, all is right in the world.

"How did we get so lucky, Zane?" I look over at him standing in the doorway.

"It's not luck, babe. It's us letting go of what was destroying us. In life, sometimes, all it takes is righting a few wrongs."

SNOOPY

"**D**aisy, get your pretty little ass behind that bar and fix us some drinks. Johnny finally got his patch, and we're fucking celebrating. You're a full-fledged member now, Nephew. Tell me, how does it feel?"

Tank has one arm around Johnny and one around Brady, smiling. It makes me happy that Prez finally got his family back, and added precious little Kennadi. He and Memphis are family men now, and it's fucking beautiful. It's times like this that make me miss my sister Asia and the life I could have had.

They killed my baby though—fucking abortion. I can't think about it tonight or I'll get angry. A drunk and angry Snoop is a bad combination.

"Shots all around, Daisy. These motherfuckers are getting fucked up tonight."

The room goes wild, filled with kut sluts and alcohol. It's gonna be a damn good night. I look over at Johnny to see him grinning ear to ear, but Tank is no longer smiling. He's on the phone with someone and it doesn't look good.

I yell for Memphis to cut the music as I make my way over to Tank. His eyes meet mine and I see pity and sadness there. Hell, I am sure that it's directed at me.

"What's wrong, Prez?" I don't even wait for him to hang up the phone.

"Dane is here. He'll be in in a second. Tell everyone to be in church in five minutes."

TANK

Fuck, just when things were getting back to normal, something like this happens to hurt one of my fucking brothers. He feels it, too. I can see it in his eyes.

Dane finally walks in, and Snoopy jumps up. "Good. You're here. Now, somebody start talking. What the fuck is going on?"

Everyone turns to look at Dane, but he looks to Snoop. "Are you sure you want me to do this here, Tank?" he asks without taking his eyes off Snoop, so of course he answers.

"I know this is for me, so stop beating around the fucking bush. These are my brothers, my family, so talk!"

Dane nods and frowns, but begins, "Well, I overheard some conversations today at the precinct, so I did my own research to make sure it was her." My brother is practically bouncing with nerves as Dane continues, "Your sister Asia is at LRMC."

"What the fuck is LRMC, Dane? What's wrong with my sister?" He's pacing the room, showing something Snoop never shows: panic.

"It's a medical facility in Germany. She was raped, severely beaten, and left for dead. Whoever done it thought they . . ." I can tell he doesn't want Snoop to panic, unsure of how much information to share.

"Tell it all, he needs to know everything."

He gives a curt nod. "In their hurry to get away, they managed to split open the skin, but she is alive and will be coming home to stay with you when released, which could take a few months. She has some broken ribs, her collarbone is cracked, and her right arm is broken."

A roar of anger rips through Snoop as he slings his chair, breaking it against the wall. "Who? Who the fuck did this to my baby sister? I need everything you can find, Dane. Don't let me down on this, brother, please."

Dane has become one of our brothers over these last couple of years. Shit has been rough and he's stayed ten toes down right with us.

"You have to know I'm working on that, Snoop. Been at it since I heard the news, but I also have something else that needs to be discussed. Fuck." He drops his head, and I know the shit about to come out of his mouth has the potential to start a fucking war. "Does the name Alina DiMarco sound familiar?

THE END

Don't worry, Snoop's book is coming up next.

OTHER BOOKS BY TISHA

The Guardian Angels MC Series

Running from Memphis
Memphis and Navy

Righting My Wrongs
Tank and Layla

Finding My Way
Snoopy and Raven:
Coming Soon

A Line Worth Crossing
Capone and Asia:
release date TBD

ABOUT THE AUTHOR

Tisha grew up in the small town of Gillsville, Georgia. She's a huge introvert, most would say all four categories. Always had a passion for writing, mostly poetry throughout her younger years. Writing her first poem in the second grade and even at that age, she was socially awkward and embarrassed to be noticed or acknowledged. She started reading and writing more as she reached her late twenties and now it has become a huge part of her life. Her heart, though, belongs to her two-year-old son, Declan. A miracle in her life that she was told she could never have. She loves her mother and father dearly and she is an only child. She has some very special people in her life. Sudie and Sarah, who read everything she writes and give her honest feedback, motivate her and push her to be better even when her depression is at its worst. She is still fighting her own demons daily, but refuses to give up.

amazon.com/TISHA-STOW/e/B08RY8HRRQ
facebook.com/authorts.stow
twitter.com/TishaStow
instagram.com/author.tisha.s.stow
goodreads.com/author/show/20963190.Tisha_Stow

A Line Crossed Is A Fate Sealed

www.ingramcontent.com/pod-product-compliance
Lightning Source LLC
Chambersburg PA
CBHW020909180626
46816CB00007BA/2320